CURSE
BREAKERS

By
Rakim Mcghee

Copyright © 2024

All rights reserved.

TABLE OF CONTENTS

Dedication 1

About The Author 2

Chapter 01 The Magic Bastard Son 3

Chapter 02 The Blessing Of A Curse 15

Chapter 03 Why I Fight! 26

Chapter 04 Unwanted Hero 39

Chapter 05 The Plan 53

Chapter 06 The Proposal 64

Chapter 07 Consequence Of The Curse 76

Chapter 08 A Bored Man And An Honorable Woman 83

Chapter 09 Calamity At The Arena 90

Chapter 10 Cursed Followers 95

Chapter 11 Who Are You? 100

Chapter 12 Brotherhood Bonds 107

Chapter 13 Friendly Fight 112

Chapter 14 The Champion's Battleground Part 1 117

Chapter 15 The Champion's Battleground Part 2 122

Author's Biography 131

Author's Note 132

Dedication

I WANT IT TO BE DEDICATED TO THE YOUNGER RAKIM, TO THE READERS, TO MY FRIENDS AND FAMILY WHO SUPPORTED ME WHILE WORKING ON THIS BOOK AND FOLLOWING MY DREAMS.

About The Author

I'M A NEW AURTHOR FOLLOWING HIS DREAM IN BECOMING A FULL TIME AUTHOR

Chapter 01

The Magic Bastard Son

In the evening, on a warm day, a father and mother with their baby were traveling along the country road back to their home when it got abnormally dark around them.

The father noticed and said, "It's too early to get this dark." Something is amiss as the baby starts crying. "Our son is crying. Calm him down, my love."

"He must be scared of the dark," his wife replied, covering the baby's eyes with her hand. "Wait, this darkness isn't real darkness, my love. We need to make haste. The cursed energy is around us. It must be one of those curse beasts around," she continued.

"I know I told you to stop the child from crying," he said. "But we must not get caught by the curse beast. They will surely try to kill us. I'll try to make some distance so you and our son can run far away, so please run as far as you can and don't look back. Take Cloud with you. He will be your guide. We will meet at the inn we planned on staying at. Okay, I love you," he kissed her wife and rushed them on their way.

Holding the baby in her arms, the woman ran as fast as she could, praying to God, "Oh God! If you hear me, please protect him and bring him back to me. I want my son to know his father and what an amazing man he is firsthand, not from stories from his drinking buddies. I pray to you to shield him with your love. O Lord, I know my husband is a great fighter, but you and I both know he can be reckless, my lord. Also, please don't let our son get that from his dad, please, lord, amen." She continued praying until she made it miles away from the fight.

"Show yourself, you cursed beast," the man said as he turned around. "I've fought your kind before. I don't know why you're here, but you picked the wrong family to mess with. This time, my two partners will be your end on this day," he added, letting out a harsh breath.

Two loud ringing sounds echoed through the air; the man shot at the curse beast that appeared out of nowhere, but the bullets had no effect. The beast struck at the man, but he dodged and threw himself out of the way, switching his bullet.

"You must be a special breed. My bullets didn't affect you. Well, no worry, I have saved something for this occasion: Magic shells!" He shouted at the beast, getting up hastily. "Let's see how you take this."

The man loaded it up as the beast flew towards him and let one off right at the beast's head. Another loud bang echoed through the air, and the beast stumbled but returned to charging at the man.

The man lets another shot off with his other gun. One more bang and the beast stumbled again but kept flying and soared towards the man. The man dodged out of the way but fell forward as something attacked him from behind him. He fell to the ground and noticed that the curse beast he was fighting didn't come alone. Another one was waiting to attack when the man didn't expect it.

"When the hell do you beasts fight in packs? You don't even look like you are the same animals," he huffed as he scrambled to get up. He realized that the cursed beasts fighting him were a Raven and a Wolf.

"Wolves sometimes hunt with Ravens, but I never considered seeing you fight together. It's not hard to believe. Well, I wouldn't let you near my family, so let's get this over with," he said, his voice laced with determination.

"Get ready. I don't have time for this. I have a family to get back to, so get the hell out of my way and die, you abominations!" he growled, his voice dripping with disdain.

Two more shots rang out, yet the curse beast swiftly sidestepped them and sent a rapid strike toward the man, sending him tumbling, his hand pressed against his side as blood started to seep out.

"We will take your son and make him our vessel; there's nothing you can do about it, human," the cursed beast snarled. "Your son has no compatibility with magic, and no spirit animal is looking to partner with him, so it makes him a perfect match for us. You can die now so we can get to him without any trouble."

Suddenly, snow started forming, and ice started attacking the curse beast, and the father got wrapped up by the earth.

"My son is too young to have a spirit animal right now, being a newborn and all. Still, it seems like someone has chosen him, and my spirit animal is here now as well. Looks like you are outnumbered now, curse beast!" the man declared.

With rekindled spirit, he reloaded his guns and aimed to shoot the curse beasts, and the spirit animals wrapped themselves around the curse beast.

One after the other, the man shot the beast until it wasn't moving anymore, but one of the cursed beasts attacked the Ice Spirit Animal, critically damaging it.

"No! You can't get away!" the man exclaimed as he fired again, but his shot missed.

The Ice Spirit chased the Wolf, which fled to finish it off. The man took out the Raven with his last shot, and the Raven's cursed energy disappeared. He and his spirit animal went after the cursed Wolf, but a howling came from the direction it ran in, and the cursed energy disappeared.

They went towards it and saw the Ice spirit lying down in the form of a fox. It showed signs of life but had taken critical damage from the Wolf.

"You helped me protect my family today, so I owe you a debt, but I have no idea what to do," the man asked. "What about you, old friend?"

"For now, let's take him with us and make a statue in his image, and you can bind him into it. He did choose to be with your son, you said, even though your son isn't capable of using magic. Maybe it's something else out there for him, and the almighty sent him to help him when the time comes," his friend suggested.

The man accepted his friend's suggestion, bound the spirit to the statue, and took it with him on the way to the inn to meet his family again. With the inn in sight, the man ran to it; his wound healed, but his clothing was still ripped.

"Did a woman with a baby boy come in here?" he inquired as he walked into the inn.

"You You're the hunter, Isaac Samuel, are you not?" the receptionist stammered.

"Yes, I am. I'm looking for my wife. We were supposed to meet here. Did she come here?" Issac asked urgently.

"Oh yes, sir, she's in the second to last room. Your son is a quiet child. He hasn't cried one time. He ate and went straight to sleep afterward," he replied.

"Well… my son takes after me in that. We like to rest after we eat, haha. They are my pride; I'll do whatever it takes to keep them smiling." Issac replied with a proud smile. "You should understand; you look like you're a father as well, am I right?"

"Why yes, sir, I'm a new father, just like you. I have a young girl. She's sickly, but she's a fighter. I know she's going to do something grand in this world," he replied warmly.

"I hope she does. She and my son shall also be good friends and help each other," Issac said with a hopeful smile.

"That would be great, sir," the receptionist agreed, sharing Issac's optimism.

"Aye, cut the sir crap. Just call me Isaac. Now, I've got to get to my family. Can I get some meat and water sent to my room to eat and join my son in the dream world in a few?" Issac requested.

"Yes, Isaac. I'll have it sent your way as soon as possible. Have a good night," the receptionist replied.

"You as well," Issac responded before heading off.

"Oh, thank you, Lord, for such a wonderful day. Who would have thought that the hunter, Isaac Samuel, would come to my inn and converse with me of all the people? He's down to earth like they say he is. Wow, he even wants our kids to be friends. That's amazing," the receptionist reflected with gratitude.

A Few Years Later

"Get up. It's time for your first training lesson, son. You're going to learn how to fight bare hand," Issac said, gently shaking his son awake.

"Dad, do I have to train this early in the morning?" his son groaned, rubbing his eyes.

"Yes, it would be best to have good habits, and getting up to work early is good. You won't have me to protect you forever, son. You must become a man who can protect himself, his loved ones, and the weak," Issac explained solemnly, emphasizing the importance of self-reliance and responsibility. "Do you understand?"

"Yes, sir, I promise to become the kind of man who can do it," his son replied earnestly, becoming more awake by the second.

"Good, now let's go before your mother wakes up. She hates the idea of you learning hand-to-hand combat," Issac chuckled.

"It's not my fault I can't use magic, like you two say. God made me this way," he furrowed his forehead.

"You're right, son. He did, and you'll have to make the best of it," Issac laid his hand on his son's shoulder. "I know you will. Let's go. We will start with a light warm-up, then you will go for an easy 50-mile run. When that is done, we will work on your fighting technique, and then you will spar. After that, we will call it a day."

"Who am I going to spar with, Dad?" he asked.

"You are going to spar with a boar bear, son. Focus, son, don't just swing to swing when you fight. You want it to feel as natural as possible. Now punch and drop down, get up, and then run. Let's go!" Issac instructed, urging his son to focus and guiding him as they began their training session.

"Move! Move! Hit! Come on, you can hit harder than that, son. Let's go full power!" Issac encouraged his son during their training session.

The young boy punched with a grunt, and a shot of energy shot out from him. "Wow! What was that, Dad?" he asked excitedly.

"Son, that's what we call an energy blast. It seems like you're developing your way to make up for not having magic so you can attack from a farther distance. That's good, especially for the first day. If you keep up like this, you'll be able to fight without magic with no problem," Issac assured his son.

"That's good, right, Dad?" his son asked, hopeful for approval.

"Yes, son, that's amazing. Okay, let's keep going. Do you still have the statue I gave you?" Issac inquired, his eyes filled with curiosity.

"Yes, sir, it asked me if we could be friends," his son replied, the excitement still clear in his voice.

"What do you think about that?" Issac asked, a smile tugging at the corners of his mouth.

"I would like that," his son responded eagerly, already envisioning the possibilities.

"Okay, son, I'll take him out of the statue, and you two can play tomorrow, alright?" Issac suggested.

"Yay! I'm going to have a new friend to play with," the young boy exclaimed joyfully.

"Yes! My son will finally have his spirit animal. It will also be off the ice element, which is rare. Still, his inability to use magic is also rare," Issac mumbled to himself, a sense of pride evident in his voice as he reflected on his son's unique qualities.

"What do you have planned for my son, and will I live to see it?" Issac asked the statue, a note of concern creeping into his voice.

"I hope so. I won't focus on that," the spirit bound in the statue replied.

"I will enjoy my time with him and my wife. Such a beautiful day," Issac said with a soft tone, living in the present moment.

Later That Night

"Son, come here!" Issac called out.

"Yes, Dad?" his son responded, appearing by his side.

"Son, can you connect with the power you used earlier?" Issac inquired.

"I can still feel it going through my body," his son confirmed, nodding eagerly.

"Good, my boy. Please focus on that energy, connect it with the energy in this statue, and try to bind the two together. Take your time. You can seriously hurt yourself if you do this wrong. You understand, right?" Issac cautioned, his voice filled with concern.

"Yes, sir, but I'm more afraid now," his son admitted, his voice trembling with apprehension.

"It's okay to be afraid, son, but you can't stay afraid forever. If you do, the world will eat you up alive. I'm not telling you this to scare you; I'm telling you this to prepare you for the world when you go out into it on your own," Issac said, tears shimmering in his eyes.

"Remember that when we are training, no matter how hard it gets, you must endure and become stronger to take on the tough challenges ahead. Life might never get easier. So, having those moments like we're having now will be rewarding. No matter how much hell I go through in the outside world, it's all worth it when I get back here with you and your mother," Issac assured his son.

"I understand what you mean, Dad. Thanks. I have confidence in doing this now," his son said, his eyes smiling.

The young boy focused, and a white aura appeared around him. The statue glowed blue with a hint of black, and then the black faded away. The mother noticed a surge of energy from the statue, and it changed from blue to black.

"Honey, why is it the ice spirit aura going black?" the mother asked, concern apparent in her voice.

"Now that I think about it, the only black aura I know of is cursed energy. But when I put the spirit into the statue, there wasn't any cursed energy around," Issac pondered aloud, his brows furrowed in deep thought.

"Wait, is it possible that the curse beast affected the ice spirit? Is that possible?" Isaac asked suddenly as the boy continued to channel the spirit. "If so, what do we do now once he starts? We can't stop unless we risk the chance of losing our son. We have to let it finish and see why it happens. We must have a sealing spell ready just in case." The urgency was apparent in his voice.

The mother chanted as the boy mixed his energy with the ice spirit. All of a sudden, the boy's energy turned gray with a blue tone, and then it disappeared. The boy fainted.

Both parents rushed to the boy. The father picked him up to check on him as the mother shouted, **"MY SON! GET UP, BABY, GET UP. ARE YOU OKAY? OH, LORD! PLEASE LET OUR SON MAKE IT THROUGH THIS!"**

"Calm down, honey. He is asleep." Isaac assured his wife, as she regained control of her heart. "It seems like doing this took a toll on him, which makes it common for a child who doesn't have a connection with magic. He needs to rest and then eat. He will be okay. Calm down."

"Oh, but when will he wake up?" the mother asked impatiently.

"I don't know; it's not the same for everyone. Do you remember how long it was before you woke up?" Issac asked, trying to gauge the situation.

"I was out for 8 hours, but if I remember, you were only out for an hour, right?" the mother recalled.

"Yes, but I was a teen when I got to merge with my spirit animal," Issac confirmed.

"You were 10, but it wasn't as important when you merged. You had a much better grip on using your abilities, but I didn't," the mother said. He realized that he would have several things to discuss with his wife and develop a strategy for their son's abilities.

"When our son wakes up, he's going to have many questions," he acknowledged, already preparing himself for the conversation ahead.

Chapter 02

The Blessing Of A Curse

The boy woke up in a dark area and found a gray-and-blue fox staring at him.

"You awaken, good, young boy," said the fox. "Come closer. I will not do you any harm. You've seen me before, have you not?"

"You're the Fox from the statue," the boy replied in shock, but he was surprisingly calm.

"Yes, your father saved me when he put me the statue in so I can rest and heal." The fox nodded and carried on in a mystical voice. "It's rare when a spirit animal gets hurt, but it's bound to happen when dealing with a curse beast."

The boy looked around suddenly, whipping his head side to side. "What is the problem that you are looking for?" Asked the fox.

"The curse beast is here. I can feel him." The boy said nervously.

"You are right." The fox said, quietly noticing the wisdom emanating from the boy. "He is here in a way. Let me explain. The curse beast has merged with me, so he also merged with you."

"What does that mean? Am I going to be a bad boy?"

"No, it means you're going to become a curse eater."

"What is a curse eater?" The boy asked with a frown. It didn't sound too good to him, and the nervous feeling in his heart was growing.

"A curse eater is a person who eats curse energy and uses it against the curse beast and other things." The fox explained. "In short, you still have the choice of if you want to do good with the power you have been given, and I came to help you. I will work more as a guide for you. I will also help you with fights as much as I can."

"But I can't use magic, and you can't help as much as if I were someone else, right?" inquired the boy.

"Yes, sorry that you have to go through that. You'll already have a hard life because of your family name. Now, being unable to use magic and becoming a curse eater will make things harder for you, but I promise to help you through it."

"My father and mother always told me that the Lord gives his strongest warriors the hardest battles. I should be thankful for this." The determination was evident in the boy's voice, resembling his father.

"I know I don't feel bad about it; I will make it through it all, no matter how hard it gets. I promised my parents and the Lord that, and I'll also make that promise to you and myself."

The fox nodded and replied, "Good. Now, about being a curse eater. You will need to eat curses to get stronger and control your powers better. Be sure not to go after too strong curses or the curse energy inside you will become too strong and take control of you, which won't be good. I'm working as a check to the current power of your cursed energy.

The stronger our bond gets, the stronger I can get to keep you in control of the curse energy. So, please rely on me when fighting. You have to use the abilities I give you and become better with them so I can grow stronger to combat the cursed energy.

"I will, I promise." The boy said hurriedly.

"Good, now, with that out of the way, what is your name, young boy, and what will you name me?"

"My name is Israel, and I'm four years old."

"Is someone so young my partner, now?" The fox asked in amusement, "Okay, what will you be naming me?"

At that question, the boy jumped up excitedly. "You are an ice fox. Can I name you Snowball?"

"Snowball, are you sure about that?"

"Yes!"

"Well, I can't say I'm surprised by the name. You are a child, after all, so Snowball it is."

"Yay!" The boy cheered.

"It's funny; you're the second person to call me that."

"Who was the first one?"

"He was the first person I ever teamed up with. He had the same name as well. His last name was Samuel."

"Wait, that's my name too! I'm Israel Samuel!"

"What! Really? What are the chances that maybe you two are family?"

"Maybe I'll ask my parents when I see them. Wait, where are my parents anyway?" The excitement in the boy's voice was fading as he worried about where he was and where his parents were.

"You will see them when you wake up. Are you ready to wake up?"

"I guess so."

"Get back into your bed and wake up. Don't worry; we will talk about more in the future after all we are one now, so we can always talk to each other. I'll talk to you later. See you soon." With those words, the fox started to disappear, and the kid felt dizzy like he was falling asleep.

The next second, he woke up back in his room. He yawned widely and sniffed the air. "That's Mama's cooking. I think it's boar. Potatoes, too. Well, friend, you and the other guy are about to have some of the best food," he said to himself, speaking to the fox in his head. He jumped out of bed and rushed towards the kitchen.

"Dad? Mama?" He called out, and with a gasp, his mother immediately turned around and rushed to him. "Som! You're up!"

"How long was I out?" he asked his father, hugging his mother.

"You were out for about three hours. How do you feel, son?" his father asked.

"Hold it before you eat, clean yourself, and then you two can discuss this," interrupted his mother. "You were raised with manners, young boy."

"Yes, Mama." Israel went to clean himself and then returned to eat.

"Now, son, how do you feel?" his father inquired.

"I feel a little sleepy but also energized simultaneously. It's hard to explain".

"That's good. Did anything happen when you were sleeping? Did you see something?"

"Yes, I got to talk to my spirit animal."

His father's eyebrows shot up. "What did he say?"

"He said I needed to learn to balance my cursed energy and his Ice power."

"You can use his ice power? How?" The curiosity was apparent in the father's voice.

"Well, that wasn't explained. I guess I will find out as I train and become stronger and bond with him."

The father nodded and sat back. "I can train you on using your spirit animal, but first, we have to find out how you can use its power.

It may work with the power we saw earlier with the energy blast you did. Maybe you can blend the two, but on to the real problem: did the cursed beast affect you?"

"Yes, it is a part of my spirit animal, so it's also a part of me."

"Hmmm. We must find a way to train you to use the cursed beast's power.

"Honey, isn't that going to be a problem?" his mother asked, expressing concern.

"Yes, my love, no one knows how to use it. Maybe we can talk to the spirit animal."

"Can we see if it can talk to us about how we train it so our son can use it to the best of his ability? Do you think that will work, honey?"

"Yes, it should. Let's call Muka. He should be able to handle this for now. Let's eat now. He will be here before we train tomorrow morning so we can get more details on this, but for now, it's family time. Let's say our thanks, eat, and go to bed. They ate, enjoyed their time together, and went to bed after saying goodnight.

The following day starts with Muka knocking on the door.

"Dad, is it the guy you mentioned last night?" Israel asked his dad.

"Yes, son, he can speak with any spirits. Sit down, and we can start soon."

"Yes, sir, and hello, Mr. Muka."

"Hello, young one. I hear you have been picked to be a curse eater. Is that true?" The man asked him calmly.

"Yes, but I don't know anything about it. I was hoping you could talk to the cursed beast affecting my spirit animal about how to use his abilities and how I can train to understand it."

"I know why I was called here. I just wanted to talk to you so you can be comfortable with me. After all, if you become uncomfortable, it will be hard to connect with the spirit because it will want to protect you, so it will become aggressive with me if you're not calm and welcoming.

"I understand, but my dad asked you here so you can speak with my spirit, so don't worry." The boy smiled.

"Okay, let's get to it then. Please hold my hand, concentrate on my energy, and stay focused." The moment the boy grabbed the man's, energy shot out from them.

The man woke up from the blue area and spotted the fox. "I know you know why I'm here. Could you help me help the boy?"

"I can't help him more than I have." It seemed like the fox's voice was coming from everywhere. "I know nothing about using the curse beast's powers. It's something we will have to learn together."

"But how when he can't even use your powers yet?"

"He will use his power."

"His power?"

"It's something those who can't use magic can do. It's something he did earlier, too. He called upon a power within. I will have an understanding of it the more I stay with him. The curse beast wanted him because of this power. Maybe it knows how to use it, but it won't talk to me."

"So, what do we do for now?"

"We can't do anything but wait and let the boy train with his father to awaken more power from within. I firmly believe the more he gets a hold of his power, the more I can find out how I can help him with my power right now. His physical strength is all he has to depend on now."

"Will that be enough?" Muka asked with concern, contemplating so many things at once.

"It's enough for training."

"I don't know how he will fair in a fight. Today is my first day of training with him. I will know what he is capable of and how I can help to improve. I will also know what to do as well."

Suddenly, there was an incomprehensible voice in the surroundings, and the ice spirit whipped around! "You! You're the curse beast! Why did you choose to speak now?"

A deep, low voice sounded all around them. "I needed to straighten something out. I needed the boy to eat so I'd become stronger. I didn't speak to you because there's nothing to say. I don't know what this boy is made of; I sense he can be a good vessel. For me, he's an empty husk of a human, so he can go farther than others with magic capabilities because he's not limited by the same limits they are. It's perfect."

"So, will you help him use your powers when the time comes?" The ice spirit shot back.

"Of course, if I don't, he will become an empty husk. The curse energy will consume him, and he will go berserk. Why isn't he here?"

Sensing that the question was directed at him, Muka answered. "Because I'm using him as a door to enter. He could have also been here if he could use his power better. He is aware of what we have been saying this whole time.

"Good to know. Aye, kid, show me the power that I know you have. Don't be scared. You can be something. You have to take your destiny by the horns and go for it. Let's put on a good show that also goes for you, Fox Boy. I want to see what you can do. I usually fight your kind. It's my first time partnering up with one, which will be exciting. Well, I'm going to rest until the training starts." The curse beast said as his voice faded away.

"Yes, I think it's time you go."

Nodding at the fox, Muka focused and returned to the room where the boy stood with his family.

"You heard everything, right, young one?"

"Yes, sir, I did. I have to wait to develop my power, and then I'll understand how to use them on the go. Is that right?"

"Yes." Muka turned to Isaac. "Hopefully, your son can adapt to what is to come regarding his powers. I believe he can. Luckily, he has you two here to help him. The Hunter and The Witch, no one expected both of you to be married, one from a noble family and the other a low life, and now you have the kid who will be a curse eater. What a tale, what a story to tell. well I'll be off. If you need me, you know where I'll be. Sorry I couldn't be too much help to you all, but like the spirits say, you will have to train and adapt. Work hard, kid."

"I will, sir."

Putting his hand on the boy shoulder, Muka went out the door.

18 years later

"Punch! Kick! Knee! Hook! Uppercut! Low kick! Side kick! Roundhouse! Now focus and blast the target!" Isaac shouted instructions as Israel put in his best while training. He shot an energy blast from his hand and legs, hitting four targets simultaneously.

"Good, you are ready for a real fight!" His father said energetically. "But I must have you not use your blast attacks. Your aim is good with it, but I would be grateful if you could save them for your emergency."

"Yes, sir, what's the mission?" asked Israel, wiping his sweat and breathing hard.

"I am sending you to help them with a Giga bear problem in the town over the river."

"Giga bear?"

"Yes, they are the second biggest size of bears. Mountain bears don't attack unless you attack them, so this is the next best thing. You will go hunt them down and take them out. It would help if you didn't have to do more than punch and kick. You can also slam them if you want. I don't care. Just kill them and get rid of them, and it will be okay."

"Yes, sir, I'll set off tomorrow. What is the town called?"

"It's called Rivershadow City." Replied his mother who had been watching the training beside her husband. "I'll give you a map and directions; don't worry. I'll also have a meal for you, my big boy."

"Thanks, Mama. I promise not to be gone long."

"It's okay. As much as I want you to live here forever, I know you will have to spread your wings someday. Let's not worry about it. Eat so you can get some rest and be ready for your mission. Don't forget the meals you were taught to make."

"Yes, Mama, I remember. I've been working on them."

"Good. Now that all is settled, let's eat." They cleaned up and ate together before the real adventure in Israel's life started.

Chapter 03

Why I Fight!

Israel traveled on a boat to the town of Shadow River City. "Father told me not to tell anyone who I was," he wondered. "But he didn't give me a name to tell them. I guess I'll have to make something up. Hmm, what should it be? I could go by an Alisa-like Shadow. Would that be to convince Fred Shadow? Ahh, Dad told me not to overthink it, and if I can't, then I can use my real name. Dad and Mama are just worried that it may be too much of a burden for me at the beginning of my adventure."

"Right now, I'll focus on why I'm doing this." He shook his head and convinced himself. "I'm a curse eater, and I have to get out and fight curses and anything else out there to save everyone and keep the peace. But what else does a curse eater do? Why do I need to eat curses?"

Suddenly, a voice inside him spoke up. He was shocked at first, but he immediately understood it was the spirit inside him speaking to him. "As a curse eater, you take on curses to set the world back on the path of balance every 1000 years. Because of human greed, hate, lust, etc., curses get stronger due to humans not having control of these emotions. A curse eater is born to bring balance back, but this is the first time a curse eater can't use magic. That's why I was attracted to you in the first place."

"Is that true?" the boy asked curiously.

"Yes, other curse eaters could use magic, but they were also attached to someone with a strong desire. You are different because you are nothing but a blank canvas. I am not saying you have no importance. You just started so young; the last youngest curse eater was in his mid-30s. I wonder why you got this gift so early, and your body didn't get destroyed. You are such an interesting case. What will you do? Will you give in to curse powers?"

The boy began to answer, but the voice continued. "Maybe the power you are meant to have with the spirits is to truly be the symbol of balance and master both powers. It's something no curse eater has done before. No one has done it before."

"How do you know this?" Israel asked.

"With me and the curse beast merging, I have his knowledge. Curse beasts are the ones who give curses to people. We are also responsible for mimics. Look, we are here in time to get ready to land. Just a heads up: I won't help you with this fight. Neither of us will; you have the strength to handle the Giga Bear alone."

"That's good to know. I will have to go to a library and find a hunter to find some information on the Giga bear." The boat reached its destination and stopped, and Israel and the other passengers, along with the captain, got off the boat.

"Captain, where is the nearest Adventures Hall and a place I can find a hunter?" Israel asked the captain.

"Are you looking to join a team?" The captain responded with a curious furrow of his brows.

"No, I'm just trying to get some information."

The captain analyzed him for a second, then nodded. "Well, go 5 miles east and then 2 miles south, and you will see the Adventures Hall. You will go right behind it and find the hunters as soon as you get there. They don't go inside the Hall unless they call it a night."

"Alright, thanks." Israel thanked the captain and handed him a silver coin as a token of his gratitude. The captain smiled immediately.

"Thank you, young man, this is my whole week of pay. Bless you, have a good life."

"Same to you, sir. Be safe on your travels, and be blessed."

Unbeknownst to Israel, people took notice of his generosity and started planning to rob him. They followed him, without him knowing a thing about their scheme.

He finally reached the Adventures Hall and walked up to the elf woman at the reception. "Hey, can you help me with something?"

The elf smiled. "Why yes, how can I help you, sir?"

"Can you give me information on Giga Boar Bears?" The elf raised her eyebrows, taken aback in surprise.

"The information is not known because we never had anyone beat them." She said, and he could see the wheels in her mind running. "We still don't know what magic works on them. We plan to send some fighters to see if physical weapons would affect it, but we don't have enough trained fighters in this town."

"I see I can help." The elf was surprised yet again at his words. "Will there be any hunters to help?"

"We don't have the money, but they want to get their help."

"How can they be that greedy? Well, it doesn't matter. I will handle it myself. Don't worry about it. When would you like me to head out?"

"Tomorrow in the morning, it's getting dark. They won't be out at this time, and going to find them at night can be risky."

"Okay, where is the nearest inn?"

"Well, this is the inn for registered Adventures. Would you like to sign up?"

"No, I'll go to one for regular people. Thanks, though."

"Okay, you can't blame a girl for trying." The elf shrugged. "Go out and down two buildings over, and you will see three ends. If you have the money, it's for three silver a night, and the other option is for ten copper a night. The cheapest one is for five stone a night. Pick one, and I'll see you tomorrow morning."

"See you then." Israel thanked her and headed out towards the inn. He walked up to the reception. "Hello, can I get a room here tonight?"

"Yes, as long as you can afford it. It's three silver and another silver for food."

"Okay, here you go." He handed the money to the receptionist.

"Thank you, your room number is seven. The buffet is down the hall to your left. Have as much as you like."

"Thank you." The moment he turned around, he saw two men and two women walking into the inn with scowling expressions.

"Hey, you!" One of the women shouted at him. She was slim and had brown skin against which her red and green dress glowed. She had straight hair, and no part of her looked attractive to Israel. She looked like a street rat. "Where are you going, thinking you're some big shot, coming here and getting a room for yourself when we have to put together money to get a room!"

"I have the money for it. That's how it works." Israel responded plainly.

The receptionist immediately called out in a strict tone. "Excuse me, if you're not going to get a room, you must go. Now!" The woman in the red and green dress looked at her group and nodded toward the receptionist as if telling them to handle her.

"Hold it right there," Israel exclaimed bravely. "You have no right to bother anyone here. If you want a fight, then step outside. I'll take you all on at once."

The group of people laughed and mocked him. "Do you think you can take us? You must have a death wish, kid." One of the men leered at him.

"If you are certain, step outside, and we can see who has a death wish."

"Okay, boy, we'll take all your coins when we win."

"No worries here. I don't plan on losing anything to you, punks." With that, Israel stepped outside, and the group followed with angry expressions, murmuring among themselves. One of them leaped forward in an attempt to catch Israel off guard, but he was ready.

"You guys aren't worth the time, but I could use this chance to stretch my muscles," Israel said, stretching his neck and arms. The thug group charged at him one by one. One of the women rushed forward and tried to round-house kick Israel, but he blocked it and sent her flying with a low kick. Then, another opponent came; a tall, slim guy ran up to him, throwing punches. Israel slipped out of the way, dodging him, then hit him with a hook, liver shot, low kick, and a back fist, sending him flying into the next man who was running up to try to fight with him.

The first woman yelled at one of her men angrily. "We're going to have to fight him together his trained in hand-to-hand combat. Let's use our magic. I notice he hasn't used any magic, so he may not be good with it. Come on, let's get him together!"

Both of them cast the twin magic of earth and wind: continental winds. A strong blast of wind and boulders shot out towards Israel.

"Oh, you are capable of using twin magic, I see. That can mean only two things." He put his guard up and punched the boulders into cobble, stood strong against the wind, and disappeared.

"Huh? Where did he go, Jess?" One of the people in the group asked.

"I don't know Roger, he just disappeared." Suddenly, Roger goes flying backward. Jess turned around and got punched and knocked into the dirt as if she was getting buried underground. The others stood and watched in shock.

"Well, that was easy," Israel said as he dusted his hands. "Now, let's eat and sleep, guardsman. Can you handle these ruffians?"

"Wow! That was too fast." One of the guardsmen exclaimed, clearly impressed. "If we had you around here working with us, this place would always be safe. Are you looking for a job?"

"No, I already have work to do. Thank you for the kind offer, though."

"Well, have a good night, and be blessed."

As Israel took off, a woman in revealing clothing approached Israel. "Hey baby, you got to be tried after that fight. Why not let me relax your body tonight?"

"No, I'm good. They didn't even make me sweat at all. Thanks, anyway. Be safe and blessed."

"Wait, baby, can't you give a girl your time? I want to make you happy if you know what I mean."

"I don't, and I said I'm good. I want to eat, clean myself, and sleep now. Goodnight." Israel started to walk away, but the woman grabbed his hand.

"Wait, baby, let me join you for the night. You can't let a woman be alone at night. It's bad people out there. You just saw for yourself, did you not?"

Israel glared at her. "Look, I don't know you. Is there a reason you insist on staying around me? If so, say it now!"

The woman's face got sad, and then she looked at Israel. "My father got caught up in debt with a bad man, and I ran away so I wouldn't get forced into being a streetwalker. I know my clothing may look like I'm doing it, but I never slept with anyone. I'm still waiting for my husband to be my first. I drug people and take their money to make them think something happened. I will be there with them in the morning and offer them food afterward. That's the truth, I promise."

"Why are you telling me? How do I know this isn't a lie? You're telling me those people wanted my coins; how do I not know if you are not with them?"

"Let's go inside, and I can prove it to you. I promise I'm not trying to trick you. I need your help."

"Okay, come, let's see if you're telling the truth, but I won't hesitate to leave you if you lie." They walked in together, and the woman waved at the woman in the front, and she waved back.

"Dee, you know this strapping young man? We just met. I saw the fight outside. Do you know why that happened?"

"Yes, those people were mad. He could buy a room by himself and wanted to fight him for his money. Childish, if you ask me."

"I agree, but I did see that our friend here is one heck of a brawler. He's so good I think he can help us."

Dee looked at the lady at the front desk as if they were sharing a secret.

"Are you sure about this?"

"Yes, Emily, I am. Very much, so I believe he will fix our problem once and for all, my friend."

Israel looked at both of them. "What are you two talking about? Please say what you must say and stop being so coy about it."

"Sorry about that, sir. What room do you have? We can talk about it in greater detail there."

Israel held his hand up. "No woman is going to my room this late at night. That is wrong. I'm not married, so no night, and I will not change my mind about this."

"Okay, I'll send it as a letter going into detail. You can give us your answer tomorrow. How does that work for you, sir?"

"That's good with me. I'm going to let you ladies go. Be safe and blessed."

Israel went to eat and took a bath before going to bed, and the ladies talked in the other room. "Dee, are you sure he will do it?"

"No, I don't know, but if you saw him fight, you would know we must try. So many women are in trouble, and we need someone skilled at fighting to help."

"You talk about him fighting. What was so special about it?"

"He fought those people without using magic, not even once, and blocked a magic attack with his fist. When have you ever seen or heard of that?"

"Dee, how do you not know if he didn't use magic to block the magic?"

"Emily, you know I can see magic. I would have noticed if he had used it."

"You have been off a few times, Dee."

"Do you remember taking the time up north? He did use magic. It just was illusion magic that's harder to detect, and you know it."

"Yeah, whatever you say, but let's say you're right. What if he hides his magic because it's not good, or maybe he cannot use it?"

"Come on, Emily, you know that it's way too rare that someone can't use magic. He would not make it past birth if he didn't use magic to some capacity."

"Look, Dee, I'm just saying let's not get our hopes up that he's the one, even if he's good at hand-to-hand combat. That's cool and all, but how would we know if it's enough we can't risk the girl's safety on this guy when we don't know him at all? Don't get me wrong, I'm sure he's a nice man and can fight, but why would anyone help people they don't know at all? It's not like he's a wannabe hero or something."

"Emily, please trust me for once on this. I know this guy will do it. I know it."

"Okay, I will trust you this! I have work to do now, so go to our room and sleep. I'll see you and him in the morning."

"Alright, goodnight."

In the morning, Dee left a letter for Israel at his door for him to read. He saw the letter, picked it up, and started reading it.

"Mr. Brawler, sir, I'm Demi, the woman you met last night with Emily. This letter asks you to help us with a problem plaguing town. Young women lose their innocence by being streetwalkers by the Thakur family. They plan to get families with beautiful young daughters into debt. To make up for the debt, they have the fathers sell their daughters or force them to work for them in their inn. There, they do whatever the highest buyer tells them to do. They are disgusting men who even impregnate some of the women. He takes and claims them as his own forever."

"My sister and I can't fight him; we're not capable of fighting him. Still, I know you can, and you can give him a good beating. We need you; it's a big prize for you if you do it. I'll be waiting for your answer in the lunchroom."

Israel balled up the paper and threw it away. "I can't do it right now. I'll have to handle this later. It would be wrong to ignore this, but I must deal with the Giga Bears first." He went to the lunchroom to eat. Demi and Emily joined him. They both looked anxious.

"Look, you two. I will do it, but I have something else I need to handle before I can help you two." They both looked shocked and started to cry.

"Thank you so much. I knew you would help. You doing this means so much to us, you don't know." They got up and bowed to him. Emily looked at Israel. "I didn't think you would do this, and I had doubts about whether you were right to do it, but I'm so grateful that you will. I pray that I was wrong about you on this. I'm so sorry. Can you ever forgive me? For not believing in you, sir. And you two, Dee, I should have trusted you. I'm so sorry."

"Please get back up in your seats and don't make a scene. I'm not too fond of attention. Let's talk more about this when I get back, okay?" He got up and started to leave.

Demi and Emily shouted, "Wait, what's your name?"

"My name is Israel. I'm sorry for not telling you earlier. Nice to meet you two officially. I'll be back after I deal with the Giga Boar Bear problem. See you later. Be safe and blessed."

"Dee, did he say he is going fight a Giga Boar Bear?"

"Yes, he did, and with a straight face, did we just ask someone insane to help us? After hearing that, it's hard to say no. If he returns, we may have to wait to save the girls."

"You may be right about that, but as long he gets it done, I don't care. Let's pray that he returns in good condition."

"Yeah, let's do that."

Israel walked out and headed to the meeting spot to meet with the other Adventures.

"The big day." He thought to himself. "The day I show why I fight! I believe the strong protect the weak. I know I won't be fighting with my all because I won't have access to anything but my physical strength, but I know I can do this. Dad, Mama, I won't let you down. I'll show you what I'm capable of here and now and become a strong hero who protects those who can't fight for themself. I'll be a shield to those without protection, hope to those who want to give up, and a ray of light in the darkness. I vow to the lord that I will never abandon my goals and dreams." He felt ready to take on anything that would come his way.

Chapter 04

Unwanted Hero

In the forest of Shadow River, warriors and wizards met to plan on taking on the Giga Boar bear. One stood out as the leader of the group, a tall European man. He looked like a seasoned vet, and next to him was the Elf girl Israel met yesterday. She noticed him and waved for him to come to her.

"Hey friend, good to see you here."

"Hello, good morning. I hope you slept well, so what's the plan?" Israel asked her eagerly.

"Could you hold it for now? We have to have you meet the head man in charge", she said calmly. "This big guy here is Sir Charles the Hammer. He is a hero from overseas who was here and kindly offered to help for free."

"Wow, isn't that nice of you?" Israel said in pleasant surprise as he turned to the man. "Nice to meet you. I'm Israel, and I'm new to the world of adventure. I'm hoping to learn a lot from you." Israel held his hand out to shake Sir Charles' hand.

"Well, you look like a strong young man. Nice to meet you, young Israel," Charles said, shaking Israel's hand with a firm grip, something you expect from a seasoned warrior like him. "I want to be a good teacher in the time we are together."

As they shook hands, he took notice of Israel's grip as well, the ghost of a smile appearing on his face. "You have a firm grip, young man. I want you on the frontline with me. I want to see what you're capable of, my friend. Could you do me this honor?"

"Ah, yes, sir," Israel responded excitedly. "Thank you for the opportunity." The older man studied him for a second, the gears in his mind turning.

"This young man has a different feel to him," thought the older warrior to himself. "I can't guess what. He reminds me of someone I used to know, but who? Well, I don't need to consider that right now. It's time for battle."

"All right, men, it's time to fight." He announced to Israel and the rest of the men gathered around him. "Team A goes to the front of the cave, and Team B goes to the back, starts the fire, and closes it off. The smoke from the fire will draw them out, and we will surprise them with a trap and then attack them when they are vulnerable."

"Now, getting to the Boar bear is going to take a lot of work. We will have to scale a mountain and then go through the deeper parts of the forest, where we will run into other creatures like giant eagles, silver foxes, killer otters, and other animals. If we walk around the mountain, we can avoid the eagles, but we will run into the foxes. If we make it through that, we can take the shortcut past them to avoid the otters and get there quicker. That will be better unless you guys want to fight more before the main event."

"Let's try to minimize the casualties as much as possible. With that said, let's be good men. It's time to fight! Let's go!"

The group of men shouted, "Let's fight!" as everyone headed out to fight the Boar bear. The elf girl waved and shouted after them, "Bye, you guys! Please come back safe!" With that, she headed back to the Adventures Hall. The group split into two teams and continued on their way. It was not long before one of the groups ran into the silver foxes. The wizards stayed in the back, and the warriors in the front. The warriors cast spells on their weapons as they approached the fox's den.

"Sir, the foxes just finished hunting and are heading back to their den. Should we wait for them to eat or attack now?" One of the warriors said to Sir Charles. "They look tired from the hunt, so it may be good to attack directly."

"You're right, but to be sure, Team Leader Chai, have your team use a spell on them to hit them from afar, and we can finish it from there."

"Good idea, Charles." Chai nodded, turning to his team. "Alright, fireball on the count of three. 1, 2, 3!" The wizards cast a fireball in sync, hitting the foxes and causing them to run out of control.

"Okay, now! Attack!" Yelled Charles, and the warriors rushed out to attack the foxes, chopping all their heads off. The whole ordeal was over in a matter of mere minutes.

"Good job, men," Charles said proudly, standing back and looking at the aftermath. "Now, we can take the path through their den. It is here, right Chai?"

"Yes, it is a straight walk from here, and we can reach the Boar bear a little before evening."

"Okay, let's go, everyone. Wizards, get to the middle so you're better protected." Charles commanded, and the group got into the ordered formation before they continued on their way to the Boar bear. When they got there, the two teams split again. The warrior team laid out a trap and signaled to the wizard team to start their part of the plan. The wizards got the fire started and covered the back exit.

"We only wait for them to wake up and run out here," Charles said as all of them stood in their places and watched the scene, eagerly waiting for the bear to come out and fall into their trap. They stood waiting, and about 30 minutes later, they heard the sound of frantic stomping, and just a few seconds later, the Boar bears ran out in a rush. One fell into the pit, but the other walked over it. As it ran, something in Israel's mind, something like a signal, went off.

"Wait, something about the one that didn't get trapped," Israel said to himself as he tried to get a closer look at the escaped bear. "What is this feeling coming over me? I am hungry."

The laughter of the cursed spirit echoed inside Israel's very being. "That's the hunger of the curse eater," spoke the beast, which only Israel could hear. "I didn't think it would happen this soon. Your first mission, and you run into something that has been cursed. You must be the one to finish this one off so you can adsorb the curse energy, and we can become stronger. We may unlock a new ability when you consume this curse. We will have to wait and see how it fights."

"Okay," Israel said after contemplating for not more than a few seconds. "Sir Charles! I want to take on the one that didn't fall for the trap."

Sir Charles was surprised, but he believed in Israel and nodded. "Okay, but not alone, no. That's suicide. At least, let me and Chai help you. Everyone, focus on the one that's down. Chai, come with me and young Israel to take the bear that's still up."

Chai nodded. "Okay, but we must be careful with that one. Something is off with that one. I can't put my finger on it, but there's something wrong with it."

Israel nodded, and the three of them charged ahead, with Israel taking the lead. "Okay, this is my time to prove myself once and for all," Israel thought as he ran and got up close and punched the Boar Bear in its huge, muscly leg. It grunted and tried to bite him, but he rolled out of the way with the agility of a ninja. Charles jumped up and bashed the bear's head with his hammer, making it stumble.

With the bear in a weakened state, Chai cast a thunderbolt spell, shocking the bear. The bear growled, the loud sound reverberating through the air, and stomped madly on the ground, causing a quake and making the three heroes fall. The bear clawed at them, but Charles put his shield up to block the attack. His shield took the hit, but the sheer force of the bear's continuous attacks. The wizards cast a cloaking spell on Israel and told him to attack the top of the bear's head, which was its weakest point.

"Do as much damage as possible! We will distract it down here!" One of the wizards shouted to Israel. He took off immediately to get behind the boar bear and jumped on top of its bulky back, climbing towards its massive head. The Boar bear didn't notice a man crawling on top of him, Israel took advantage of the fact, crawling towards its neck. As he got there, the bear felt something on its neck and immediately slashed at it with its claw. The massive claw almost caught him, even when invisible, but barely dodged him and ran towards its head.

Instantly, he started delivering heavy blows to the bear's head, and as he watched and hit, the Boar bear started to get weak in the legs. It struggled to fight and get the invisible things off of him, but Israel started hitting harder, and soon, it fell. While it was sinking like a massive hill crumbling to the ground, it managed to grab Israel in his scarily large paw.

Chai immediately rushed to Israel's help and cast a great storm, and Charles unleashed a vicious hammer strike to the bear's arm with

Israel in it, freeing him. "With me, Israel!" Charles shouted. "Let's combine our strengths to finish this one off in one blow!" Israel focused all his energy, and a gray aura with a blue tint surrounded his hands and feet as Charles yelled, "Now! Attack!"

The Boar bear had managed to get up. It roared in pain and anger and ran towards them. Feeling its cursed energy, Israel attacked with all his might, with Charles' hammer glowing sliver and striking the ground, replicating the quake the Boar bear created. The hammer blow made a hole in the ground, and the bear stumbled into it. Israel jumped forward and landed a kick on the bear's head, driving it into the ground more. Charles pummeled the Boar bear until it stopped making noise, and they were covered in blood.

With heavy breathing, they looked at the bear until they were sure that the bear was finished. Charles then said, "Now that's how we men fight a beast until we or it is the only one standing." The whole group cheered in victory. Charles turned to Israel.

"Great job, Israel. What was that magic you were using there? It looked amazing."

Israel smiled and said, "If you want to know, we must talk about it privately." Before Charles could respond, Chai walked up to Israel with a frown. "Hmm, young man, we need to talk. First, I have questions about the power you used when we return." He got up closer to Israel and muttered. "Rid this beast of the curse first if you are what I think you are." With that, he walked away, leaving Israel in shock.

Charles watched him walk away, then turned and told everyone that it was time to go. He then turned to Israel. "Thank you for your cooperation, young hero." He shook his hand and walked up to Chai, towering over him

"What did you ask him to do?" He inquired, his eyes holding all the seriousness in the world.

"If he is who or, better yet, what he is, it's best we let him be alone for a little bit," Chai informed him. "I will fill you in on it on our way back. Everything will be okay. After all, we know his father and mother."

Once everyone left the area, Israel focused, and the curse beast and the Fox spirit came out. The cursed wolf said, "So he knows who you are. Did your father tell them about you and us?"

"I don't know," Israel said, confused. "But they must be someone my parents trust if he did. I would say so."

The Fox spirit spoke up. "Now, about the curse on the Boar bear, what do we do to rid it of the curse?"

The Wolf smirked. "We eat it, of course.'" The Wolf turned to Israel to show him how to eat the curse. "Put your hand here and let your curse energy, which is me, eat it, and let's see what we can get from it. Come."

Israel touched the cursed Boar bear, and a surge of curse energy consumed him, and then he blacked out. Not knowing where he was or what state he was in, Israel started seeing a film playing in front of him. He saw the curse being used by a past user before the Boar bear got it.

"You see the human who had this curse before the Boar bear got it?" The curse beast spoke from all around him. "It seems like an older man had it. Let's see how he uses it to see what it is." The film continued before him, and in it, the older man stepped into a shadow and returned home.

"So, is this a way to travel, like teleporting or something?" Israel asked the curse beast.

"Yes, it's called Shadow Walk. With this curse ability, you can travel through darkness to anywhere in the area or anywhere you have been before when you become more used to it."

"I can teleport through shadows now?"

"Yes, that's a simple way of putting it."

"That's cool. I like that. I can use that in battle to take advantage of my enemies."

"Now, let's return. You're going to have to train to use this. It's not something you can use now. You have to rest so your body can adjust to the power first."

Israel set on his way back, but not too late after he started going back, he heard someone following him. He whipped around and called out, "Who is there?"

A woman came out of the bushes, smiling. "Hello, are you Israel?"

"Yes, I am. Who are you?" He asked skeptically.

"I'm Millie. My father told me to get you and walk with you on the way back. Is that okay with you?"

"Why?"

Millie laughed. "Oh my, he didn't tell you? My father and your father, as well as Sir Charles, are close friends, so it's only right that I, his oldest daughter, would be the one to have you escort me back. We are close, you know, because our family is close, why don't we continue that relationship?"

Israel looked confused, then relaxed. "I have no problem with this. Let's leave here before it gets too dark, lady Millie."

Millie reached her hand out. "It's a pleasure to meet you, Israel."

"Likewise, lady Millie." Israel took her hand and kissed it. They walked and talked on the way back to Shadow River City.

"So, Israel, how does it feel being a Curse Eater? Are you hungry now for a curse, or did the one you ate fill you up? Do you get any abilities from the curses you eat? How many have you eaten?"

"Wait, wait, one question at a time." Israel held his hands up. "I haven't eaten one before today. Also, I'm not sure if I will get something each time I eat a curse, but I did this time. Although, I can't use it until I rest for a bit."

"Wow, that's cool. One more question: how is it that you have a spirit animal but can't use it? What is the point?"

"It's working to keep me from being controlled by the cursed beast inside me. That's what I heard, at least." Israel said with a shrug.

"Oh, okay, that sounds cool. Do you think you can handle all the pressure you'll get if other people discover it?"

Israel hummed. "Yes, this was a gift given to me by the lord, so I must be able to handle it."

Millie looked at Israel with an impressed expression. "I like how you answered that. I have hope and believe you will, and I promise I will be there for you now."

"That's a lot of support for someone you just met," Israel said, suppressing a smile.

"I know, but you remind me of the stories my father told me about your father when they were adventuring together when they were younger."

"Do you think I'm like my dad?"

"Yes, I do. You're just as driven as my father said he was. I like that a man who knows what they will do and does what he says he will do."

"Thanks for the compliments."

Millie looked at Israel, stunned. "Wow, it's not fazing you."

"What do you mean?" Israel turned his head to look at her, still walking.

"I'm not used to this," Millie explained. "Usually, a guy would try to flirt a little bit back when a woman compliments him so much, but you just let it roll off like it's nothing. Why?"

"It's because I can tell you don't mean anything you say," Israel smirked. "You're trying to get a reaction out of me, so why would I give you the one? I'm not wasting my time with that, especially with someone who hasn't even told me their real name."

Millie stopped in her tracks and stared at him in surprise. "What do you mean? Of course, I told you my real name is Millie, the daughter of Chai."

"That's not your dad," Israel said with a raise of his eyebrow. "You two look nothing alike."

"Just because we look nothing like each other doesn't mean I'm not his daughter," she said, bracing.

"Yes, it does. Everyone knows if you slit someone's face into two, you'll see their father and mother's faces. When I do that to you, I don't see that, so you can't be Chai's daughter."

"That old myth isn't true," Millie said with a scoff.

"Really? If not, then let's make a bet."

"A bet? What kind of bet?"

"I bet all the money I have now and the money I'll get for completing this mission that you're not Chai's daughter. If I'm wrong, it's yours. If I'm right, I get to have you for the night." Israel challenged.

"Excuse me, what do you mean to have me?" Millie scowled.

"Just as it sounds. You'll be mine for the night to do as I please. Deal?"

Millie scoffed again. "When we are almost back, we go to the end and meet with my father in the morning. I'll get someone else to get you. I've had enough of you."

Israel laughed, sure of himself. "Okay, we are here now. I'll see you at your "father's" place. Good night, Millie."

Millie rolled her eyes and marched ahead, Israel following calmly.

Chapter 05

The Plan

Tired from the battle, Israel returned to the inn, where Emily greeted him. "Hello, Israel, you look tired. Are you still going up to help us?"

"Yes, Emily, I will. When will we start?" Israel asked, pulling himself together.

"When you come down tomorrow night, I will guide you on where we will go. We will talk more about the plan then." Emily informed him.

"Okay, see you then. Goodnight, Emily."

"Goodnight, Israel."

The warrior spent his night resting, and soon, the morning came. There was a knock on Israel's door. "Who is it?" He called out.

"It's Millie!"

"I don't know any Millie. I never met her." He responded. At the other end, it got pretty quiet.

"Please, open the door so we can talk about this. Lord Chai wants to see you."

Israel got up and opened the door. Millie came in and shut it. "Look, go with me to see Lord Chai, and please be careful and don't say I'm not Millie out loud. I promise that Lord Chai and I will explain everything later, so please come with me."

Israel contemplated for a moment before he nodded. "Okay, let's get moving. Lord Chai has questions for me anyway; I'm sure he knows the answer already. His home is farther away from here."

Emily and Demi saw Israel with Millie and were shocked, then ran over and bowed. "Israel, why didn't you tell us you knew lady Millie?"

They turned to Lady Millie. "Hello, you are as beautiful as ever. The sun is no match for how bright you shine; your hair is as beautiful as ever, and your skin is as lovely as always. You're perfect; we shouldn't be looking at you. It's an honor that you blessed us with your beauty. The gods do have favorites."

Millie responded, "You flatter me. Thank you for the compliments, but how do you know my friend Israel? Can I ask?"

"Oh, well, we asked him for some help. It's nothing someone like you should get involved with."

"Can I help you with anything?" Millie raised her eyebrows.

"We are sure your friend here is enough to help us with this problem." They responded humbly.

"Feel free to let me know if there's anything I can do."

Israel looked at Demi and Emily. "You two don't have to talk at the same time. You both know that, right?"

"Oh, you are so silly, Israel. Go with your friend. You two should spend some time together. We'll see you later."

They walked away quickly and nervously. "Okay, we can continue," Israel said as he watched them go.

Millie nodded. "Yes, let's." Both of them walked out and entered the carriage to Chai's home.

"We are here. Wait, I didn't expect Lord Chai to be waiting out front." Millie rushed out of the carriage to greet Lord Chai. "Hello, Lord Chai; I brought your guest here." Chai signaled for Israel to come to him.

Israel walked up to him. "Hello, Lord Chai, if that's what I can call you."

Chai laughed and responded. "No, call me Uncle Chai. Your father and I are brothers on the battlefield, and then we became brothers. I haven't seen you in years. You were a baby when I last saw you before your father's last battle. How's your mother? Has she been good?"

"She's good as always," Israel responded with a humble smile.

"Good, now on to business. I need to ask you for a favor. Come inside so we can talk more. I am comfortable with this. If you are hungry, we can have something made for you."

"I can go for some meat. Can we make that happen with any drink? Ale will do."

"No problem now, the lady you see here is an appearance of my daughter." He turned to Millie. "Turn back into yourself." The woman pretending to be Millie changed to a slender woman with pale skin.

"Hello, Lord Israel. I am Apsara. Nice to truly meet you."

Israel looked shocked. "I didn't expect that, and I'm not a lord. Just call me by my name."

"It would be out of line for me to be friendly with you when we are not close."

"Well then, I command you to call me by my name, Apsara."

Chai looked at Apsara and said, "He got you there."

"Yes, Israel, I will call you by your name as you wish." She whispered a 'thank you' to him.

"You don't have to whisper; it's okay."

As they were sitting inside, Chai told Israel that he needed his help with finding his daughter.

"Why do you want me to find your daughter?" Israel inquired.

"Because she was taken by a cursed warrior and had a curse placed on her. I can't track her, but I know curse eaters can track curses and be tracked by them, so you're perfect for the job."

"I see. I will do it. But I don't know how to follow curses when I'm near them. I can sense them; I never tried to follow them before. I will try. I can see what happened if I knew where she was last."

"I will have Apsara take you there if that helps you."

Suddenly, the curse spirit inside Israel spoke to him. "There is a chance that the curse will still linger, but it will be a weak scent. The closer we get to it, the easier we can track it."

Israel acknowledged that mentally and then spoke out loud to Lord Chai. "I need to know what happens to her. Did she get kidnapped?"

"Yes, she and Apsara were out on a walk, and they got attacked. Apsara, what did the attacker look like?"

Apsara flinched with fear. "It was a werewolf. It was tall with sharp teeth, a vicious smile, eyes that pierced your soul, and claws that looked like they could rip through any armor. He attacked me but wouldn't touch Millie. When I tried to get close to her, it slashed at me and then threw me away. When I went back to the spot, they weren't there. What could he want with her?"

Chai calmed Apsara down. "Let's not think about that. Israel will get her back, right?"

"Yes, I need to deal with another problem first, then I'll be ready."

Apsara glares at Israel. "What could be more important than finding Lady Millie?"

"I'm not saying anything is more important than anything. I promised to help the two women we met earlier with a problem they are having in another city tonight. I will not return on my word; my word is a sacred vow. I can't take it back when I give it to someone."

Apsara started to get mad. "What is it you told them you will do?"

"I'm going to help then take down the Thakur family who made other families' daughters be forced into being servicewomen.

Both Chai and Apsara looked shocked. "The Thakur family is back?" Chai said. "I didn't know of this; I ran them out of here years ago with your father. I'll help you with this. It will be much easier to run them out of town, but more is needed this time if all they will do is go to another city."

Israel raised his eyebrows in surprise. "Are you suggesting we kill them?"

Chai nodded. "It's the only way to deal with them once and for all. You may be against it, but there is no other way."

Israel looked down for a minute to think, then back up. "I hate that it has to come to this, but I can tell people like them who would do this to these families aren't the type you can talk out of things, so I'm willing to do what it takes to stop them even if it means killing them."

Chai nodded once again. "I will help you with your problem tonight so you can find my daughter. How does that sound?"

"It's good for me. I will let them know when I return to the inn.

"No, have them come here. It's better if we all are together and make a plan with everyone here, okay?"

"Okay, that works well. I'll get them and bring them here."

"Good, see you later, Young Israel. Be safe heading there and back."

"Thank you, sir. Be blessed."

Israel returned to get the girls and brought them to Chai's home. They walked in nervously.

"Hello, I'm Demi."

"Hello, I'm Emily. Thank you for having us in your home, Lord Chai." They bowed deeply.

Israel tapped them on their backs. "It's okay to drop the formalities. He will help us with the problem we are dealing with tonight."

Demi shot up. "You will? Thank you so much, Lord Chai! I know the girls will be happy when they see you."

Emily hugged Israel tightly. "Thank you, and I'm sorry for not believing in you before. You're a good man, and I will trust you fully from now on."

Israel hugged back. "Thanks. I will do my best to show you that your trust in me isn't in vain, Emily. Now, let's make a plan to handle the Thakur family."

They set on working on their plan for a while. "We got the plan down," said Lord Chai. "Now, let's execute it, everyone!"

Demi and Emily went ahead of Israel and Chai. "In Bangkai, a group of men and two women walk around the leader in the middle, swinging his sword around and cutting the air in two."

When they reached the Thakur family's location, they saw the men hanging around and leering at the women passing by. One of the brutish men said, "It feels so good to be king of the town. Oh, this is good."

Another guy spoke up. "Yeah, boss, you are the best."

"I know I am, isn't that right, ladies?"

"Yes, baby, you are the best," said one of the women lingering around them. Three beautiful women walked by, one an elf woman with long golden hair and a short slender body and bust, the other a taller curvy reddish brown woman with black hair and hazel eyes, and last, a pale beauty with curly black hair and brown eyes.

One of the men, who seemed to be the boss, called out, "Well, hello there, ladies. How about you come over here and play with uncle Abhisit for a little bit? I've been looking for some new wives, you three fit the bill perfectly."

Suddenly, he saw Demi and Emily followed by Israel, Chai, and Apsara. He frowned as he saw Demi and shouted towards her. "Have I seen you somewhere before?"

Demi shook her head. "No, you must have me confused with someone else, sir."

"Sir? Do I look that old to you, my love? I'll let you know I got a lot of life in me. Come and see, and your friend can join."

"No, our father wouldn't like that, and our big brother would kill you if he knew how you were talking to us."

"Oh, I think I can take your brother." The man scoffed.

"Well, if you can, then you can have us." Israel stepped forward and called out.

They all laughed among themselves before the boss spoke again. "We know you're going to lose, so it doesn't matter. When do we fight?"

"First, you must win a drinking game against us," Emily said. "If you win, you go against our father and brother. Is that a deal?"

"Yes, it is. I will win and make you three a part of my family. Get ready, ladies."

Apsara gestured for the men to follow them. "We will go to our home to start the drinking competition. Are these people a part of your accomplice?"

"These are my family members: my two daughters, Mimi and Jewel. They are the most beautiful women my family has to offer. If I lose, which I won't, I'll have to see if I can talk with your father and brother about your brother marrying them. I also have my brothers here. You can tell us your names at the wedding; let's go."

Laughing and jeering, the Thakur family followed Israel's group. When they arrived, Chai led them into an empty house and into a room. "Welcome to my home. Don't let the emptiness fool you. This is the drinking room. We don't put a lot in here because we don't need anything more than a drink and a seat."

The Thakur family looked around and dismissed the comment quickly. Chai continued, "With that out of the way, I know why you're here. You're trying to earn my daughter's hand in marriage. You're not the first, nor will you be the last, to do this. Let's get started so you can leave empty-handed like the rest that tried to challenge us."

Abhisit held his hand up. "Wait, I have an offer myself." He looked at Israel. "You have a strong-looking son here. He will be a great warrior. I want to add my daughters to this. If you win, your son can have my daughters as his wives."

Chai thought about it, looked at Israel, and looked at Abhisit's daughters. "We will let them in, but after my son has his time with them, we will see if they are worthy of being his wives. How does that sound to you?"

"I will agree to that. With that out of the way, let the drinking start."

Chapter 06

The Proposal

The drinking began. Both of them had big jugs of ale. Chai drank his slowly, and Abhisit drank his in one big, fast gulp. It was like the tortoise and the hare racing. After ten bottles, Abhisit's face was red, and he started slurring his words. Chai, on the other hand, looked the same as when he started. Abhisit's son noticed and stopped the contest.

"There's no way you're drinking ale," he exclaimed. "Let me see your bottle."

Israel stepped forward. "You're not allowed to get in the middle of this. Stand back and let them finish it, or we will have to handle it in the next room."

Abhisit's other son walked forward. "If that's the case, let all three of us go there."

Israel looked at both the brothers. "I don't plan on going easy on either of you two."

Abhisit noticed the commotion and told them to stop. "You boys are making me look inadequate around friends. Stop it now." He shouted.

The more petite boy stepped back, but the giant one shook his head and said, "No, I will not. They are cheating, and I will not have it!" As he said that, he swung at Israel. Israel nimbly moved out of the way and delivered a hook to his liver, causing the young man to ache in pain. The other brother jumped in and grabbed Israel. The taller man ran up and threw a fury of blows at Israel.

Israel flipped the little brother around, so he was the one getting hit by his brother. The petite brother shouted, "Stop hitting me! Look when you punch!"

Israel threw the little brother at the older brother, and they fell. They got up angrily and started casting a spell, but Abhisit immediately stopped them. "Don't you dare stop this now."

But the brother had already cast the spell. There was a flash of light in the room. Chai looked at Abhisit, still calm as ever. "Your sons are rude brutes, and they will pay with their lives for the disrespect they have displayed when I've done nothing but been hospitable to you and your family."

Abhisit, in a drunken state, straightened up and looked at Chai in the eye. "Do you think I didn't know it was you the whole time, Chai? I'll never forget the face of the man who embarrassed me all those years ago. You really thought I'd believe you had a son that looks like that. Do you take me for a damn fool? I kept tabs on you, your daughter, and your wife. It's no accident they both went missing."

As Chai listened to him, stunned, Abhisit laughed cruelly and continued, "Do you want to know where they are? They're both in the same place, but you're not going to get both of them alive. Only one of them will live, and you'll be the reason why."

Chai's expression instantly morphed into anger. "What do you mean?"

"Because Chai, you have to pick if your daughter is going to live, which means killing your wife, or if you will save your wife, which means letting your daughter get cursed and killing her so your wife can be free of the curse. Either way, I win in the end because you will lose. So, what will it be, Chai?"

"You might be wrong, Abhisit," Chai said. "I have an ace up my sleeves. I will have my family back. The only sad thing about it is you won't live to see it." With that, Chai immediately hit Abhisit with a wind strike. "Now, let's end this once and for all; I have a family to get to."

Chai and Abhisit broke out into a full fight while Israel fought the sons. Israel dodged the magic blast, getting up close, and grabbed one of the brothers. He threw him at the other and pummeled them to the ground. "I'm going to make this fast," Israel said with disdain. "You two are not worth my time. I have more important things to do." He focused his energy and hit the brother on top. The ground shook with the impact, and both the brothers were killed.

Chai flew above the ground using his wind element power, then used his wind spear pillar to attack, striking Abhisit, ripping him apart, and killing him in an instant. As the dust settled, Abhisit's daughters ran into the room, shocked. "What happened?! Why have my brothers and father died? What happened?"

Chai looked at the girls. "Is he your father, or did he trick your real birth parents into selling you to pay off their debt?"

The girls looked at him in shock for a few seconds, and then they started crying. "He killed our partners, and we were his daughters for eight years. Now, he's dead. What will we do?"

Israel walked up to the girls. "You will live your life the way you want to. I will take responsibility for you ladies until you can get married to a good man. Chai, can you find them work and a place to stay? I'll pay for them to stay at the hotel.

"I will find them work, but for now, let's burn these bodies and go home," said Chai. "I have got news that Abhisit is behind my wife and daughter's disappearances. I will need you to eat the curse that plagues my wife. If what Abhisit says is true, then she's the cursed monster that has my daughter captured, and she's going to try to use her as a vessel to get rid of the curse. I don't think my wife is aware of what she's doing. She loves our daughter. It must be the curse doing this to her. I know it, so it's the only way this makes sense." Chai's expression was one of anguish as he tried to make sense of the situation.

They burned the bodies; the daughters were quiet the whole time back but clung on to Israel as they left.

"Let's get some rest, everyone," said Israel. "I'll head out first thing in the morning to go get Millie and her mother and bring them back home."

"Israel, when you get my daughter, I'd like for you to help her with her journey," Chai said. "In other words, when you save her, I'll have someone meet you halfway back to get my wife, and you and Millie will go to fight the curses around the world. There are curse beasts in different places, and you being a Curse Eater, it's very important to have you do this job. Your ability to eat curses will help a lot. I know eating curses can have a negative effect along with positive, but you don't have to eat all of them. My daughter knows how to purify curses, so you two will work well together, I'm sure of it."

Israel nodded his head. "I will do my best to achieve this goal and help your daughter fight against the curses. I promise that."

Chai nodded. "Thank you, young Israel."

Israel got everyone to their places safely, and they went to rest. The next morning, Israel woke and headed to Chai's house to gather information on where to find his daughter, Millie.

"So, they were at a lake, and the monster ambushed them and took Millie away, but you have no idea where?" Israel inquired.

"Yes, the monster left some tracks along the way, but they go cool after a while. Do you think you can track it when we get to that area?" Chai responded.

"Yes, I can, but do be warned that if it's strong enough, it can track you as well, and if it's smart, it will trap us."

"It will be wise to remember this for future encounters with curses, specifically Curse Beasts and humans who can use hexes. They will be a problem well." Chai warned. "When it comes to people who use hexes, they don't touch family. You will never know how that will turn out if you hex a family member. If you have a family member with a strong connection to hex magic, they more than likely put a protection spell on you to protect you from weaker hex users. When we become closer, I will know all about your bloodline, so I'll be able to know if you do have a connection to any hex users. But let's not worry about that for now." Chai clapped him on the shoulder.

The Ice Spirit inside Israel spoke to him. "Israel, when you fight this curse beast, I'm going to help you. The more you hit it, the more you will slow it down till it freezes. The stronger the hit or the more damage the curse takes, the more effective the freezing becomes."

"I like that," Israel said as he considered the information. "But why can't I use both of you in this fight?"

"Because we are complete opposites, we will not work together that easily. It will take time, and we will need time for you to adapt to our powers. You will have to wait till we can work together and just rely on your power. You can already eat curses and gain strength from them, and you can now freeze your opponents. You're getting stronger; just wait for more."

"Spirit, forgive me if I sounded ungrateful. That's not how I wanted to come off as I just have this feeling like I'm learning myself again, like I'm training with my father again, always learning and seeing more things I can do. It's scary but thrilling at the same time. I'm just trying to get a better understanding of it all.".

"It's okay, young one, but let's focus on the task at hand and save this family."

"Yes, you're right. Let's go." Israel headed to the river and followed the marking left by the beast.

"So, this is where the marking ended; let's try to track it." He spoke to the Spirit inside him.

"Okay, Israel, focus and try to feel for the curse energy to track the curse beast."

As he focused, Israel's vision turned black, white, and gray, and then a sea of red flashed through the air.

"Israel, that's the Curse energy you're seeing. The scent is strong, which means the beast must be near. Be careful."

"Can you tell me how strong it may be?"

"I don't know because I don't know if Chai's wife was able to fight the curse for any amount of time. This could be a pure curse or a new curse; we won't know till we get there."

Israel walked on carefully, paying close attention to his surroundings to prevent a sneak attack, and followed the red trail that would lead him to the beast. He ended up in front of an abandoned-looking home and checked around it.

"Nothing on the outside; let's look inside; it must be hiding in it because the trail ends here. This could be a trick, though. Maybe I could try to open the door. I know I can punch it open and see what happens."

Israel's focus glowed gray with a blue hue as he punched the door and broke it. When the dust settled, he saw nothing but darkness.

"This does not make any sense." Israel frowned, but all of a sudden, the house disappeared. Behind Israel, the beast leaped out and attacked Israel. Luckily, Israel managed to jump out of the way at the last moment.

"Ah, you!" Israel exclaimed as he brushed himself. "I was looking for you. Let's dance, my friend."

The beast growled and rushed towards Israel, slashing at him with lightning-quick attacks. Some landed, and some missed. Israel received several cuts, but he managed to get himself together and struck the beast with a fury of punches, kicks, elbows, and knees.

He grabbed the monster and slammed it on the ground. The beast let out a roar of pain and lashed out, slashing at Israel again, then landed a powerful shot to his guts. Israel got thrown back. Suddenly, the monster's voice changed and said, "Leave me and my daughter alone, you monster."

Israel looked at the monster in utter surprise. "Have you looked in the mirror? I'm not the monster here; you are! Where is Millie? Her father is looking for her."

Suddenly, realization washed over him. "I know you are Chai's wife; you've been cursed. I'm going to rid you of it, Lady Anong, just you wait."

Suddenly, the monster spoke in a voice laced with agony. "Millie is not too far; if you can't save me, please save her."

"I will save both of you," Israel promised, but Anong's voice changed again as the monster took over and attacked Israel.

"She's fighting for control," said Israel to the spirit inside him. "It seems like the more I fight it, the weaker it gets, but this ice effect is not taking its toll. This curse is still going at the same speed; I'm going to have to go harder."

The beast headbutted Israel, stunting him and then slamming him. Israel elbowed the beast, followed by an uppercut, and got up.

"Lady Anong must have been a good fighter, but I can handle this easily." Israel powered up and surrounded himself with a vivid aura around him. The curse beast got excited as if it was loving the chance to fight Israel. They clashed at high speed, the beast slashing at Israel and Israel punching, kicking, elbowing, and kneeing the monster. Israel landed a destructive elbow to the face of the beast, and then the air around Israel got cold. Ice started to form on the beast's face where Israel hit.

Israel changed his stance and started shuffling around, then dodged the slash from the best and landed a hard hook. He hit the beast in the liver, and ice formed on that spot, too. Israel changed his stance again and started kicking the same spot. The beast started getting slower and having a harder time dodging the hit. It sluggishly attempted to hit Israel but missed.

The cursed spirit called out to Israel, "Do me a favor and hit this thing in the gut, but only with my curse power. I can break the curse now that it's weakened some, and I'll eat some of it. That should break the curse this woman was hexed with. I can't eat it by normal means, so we will have to destroy the hex completely. Don't hit too hard because the hex can leave her body at any time, and the hit might hurt her instead. Unlike curses, hex users can remove a hex before it's destroyed."

"Okay, I got it; thanks for letting me know." Israel tried to tap into his curse energy, struggling to control it. Israel punches the beast and almost obliterates the hex. Lady Anong got released by the hex but got critically hurt in the process, falling lifeless on the group with wide eyes. Israel snapped out of his focus, shocked. "Has she died?

No, this can't be! What did you do? You tricked me. I thought you were going to help me!"

"I did help you," replied the cursed spirit. "But like I said, hexes don't work the same as curses. When someone gets hexed, the hex takes over the person. The fact that she was able to talk for as long as she did was shocking."

"You're telling me you knew we couldn't save her from the beginning?" Israel said, enraged.

"No, I didn't know if she was hexed or cursed from the beginning because both have similar energy, but as you fought it, I knew. When you fought that boar earlier, I was able to eat some of its energy to help you keep your energy levels high so you can fight. I couldn't do the same with this; you had to break it for me, but you didn't have the proper control of curse energy to be able to use it solely.

The ice spirit spoke up. "I believe you can use both of us at the same time because we balance each other out at the same time, so you don't get overpowered. Also, your power works as a facilitator to help in that balance; it keeps us from going crazy unless, like just now, you try to use only one of us at a time."

"We have to take her home," Israel said, filled with remorse. "But first, let's get Millie; she's not far from here. She's a mile south from here; I can feel her divine spirit. I hope Chai will understand this."

Israel was shaken up about what happened as he headed to rescue Lady Millie. He knew he was going to have to get over it; casualties were a part of the battle, and that was a truth a warrior must endure, but he couldn't shake himself. For now, he kept moving.

Chapter 07

Consequence Of The Curse

Down the road from where the fight took place, a slim, beautiful woman, Millie, with long black hair and light tan skin, was tied up with an enchanted chain. She was muffled but trying to yell out for help. Just a little distance away, the moment Israel defeated Among, the young woman's restraints disappeared, and she fell to the ground in shock. An image of her mother flashed in her brain.

"My darling daughter," said her mother's voice in her mind. "I can't keep holding this hex that's on your back. I need to tell you if these restraints disappear, don't hold a grudge against the person who frees you. I want you to live and enjoy your life. We were put in this situation, and we had to make the most of it."

A feeling of horror filled the woman's heart as the words continued. "I hate the idea of not being with you anymore, but you have your father and your future husband to live for now. Please remember that I love you, and I always will. I wish I could say more, but I'm losing control."

The moment her mother's voice dissipated, Millie realized what had happened, her heart broke and she started crying in silence.

"Millie! Where are you?!" Millie heard someone's voice calling out to her in the distance. "Millie, I'm here to bring you home!"

Israel came into her view and she immediately stood back, getting in a defensive stance. Israel immediately stood straight and held up his hand, explaining. "Your father asked me to come to save you and your mother. I'm sorry to say but your mother...Your mother is dead."

"I know!" She shouted. "And I also know you are the one who did it!" A fireball shot out from her, hitting Israel in the chest. He fell with a grunt.

"Millie! What are you doing? This isn't what your father wants." Israel groaned in pain, getting up.

Millie walked towards him. "You killed my mother and then have the audacity to talk about what my father would want? Who do you think you are?"

The moment she got a better look at Israel, she stopped in her tracks, her anger cooling down instantly. "Wait, I think I know who you are. Are you…. Are you Israel? The son of the Hunter and the Witch?"

"Yes, I am!" Israel exclaimed.

"Oh no. I'm so sorry. I was so mad, and I hurt you. Let me heal you." Millie touched Israel and healed his wounds. It's been a while, Israel. You may not remember, but we used to have play dates when we were younger."

Israel looked at her with a mixture of confusion and surprise. "I'm sorry, I don't remember this at all, Millie."

Millie smiled. "It's okay. Your father didn't allow you to have many visitors because he wanted you to focus on your training, so I couldn't visit as much. Plus, he told my dad that he didn't want you to be distracted with girls at a young age, whatever that means."

"Oh. Well, I'm still sorry about your mother. It's my fault she's not going to make it back with us."

"She told me that if I got freed, it would be because she died, so when I got freed, I lost it and attacked you. If there is anyone who should be sorry, it's me. I acted out of emotions. I'm lucky you didn't try to get even, or I'll be a goner." Millie ended the sentence with an awkward laugh. She pointed at the spot where she hit Israel with the fireball. "You took that fireball better than I would have expected. You're one tough guy."

Israel laughed back. "It comes from my mother attacking me with magic. I can tank a hit or two, but after that, I'm in trouble. Let's get you back home so we can explain everything to your father."

Millie nodded. "Okay, let's go."

As they started walking back, Israel noticed something shining on the ground. "What is that?" Israel frowned and walked closer. There was a necklace on the ground, and he picked it up, examining it closely.

"Was this your mother's?" He inquired.

"Yes!" Mille said in surprise. "It was a necklace I was going to get from her before all this happened. Every woman in my family gave it to their daughter as a gift. It brings luck and is good for chanting to the person wearing it so they can find a good husband and raise a healthy family. I'm at a marriageable age, so I was supposed to get it from my mother in hopes of finding a husband fast."

"Here, take it." Israel handed her the necklace. "I know I'm not your mother, but I do hope you find that lucky man soon."

Millie blushed and smiled. "I think I may already have, sir Israel. Turn around, please, sir Israel."

Confused, Israel turned around, and Mille jumped on his back. "I'm exhausted. Can you please carry me home? I'll make you some homemade Gaeng Daeng; how does that sound to you?"

Israel shrugged. "Sure, I'll take it. I like home-cooked meals. Nothing can beat a meal homemade with love; it is always the best."

Millie blushed when he said, "Hold on tight, Millie, I'm going to move fast."

Millie tightened his grip, and Israel started running. Millie's hair was blowing in the wind as she held tightly onto Israel and yelled, "How can you move this fast? You're human, aren't you?"

"Yes, I am. I'm a human who can run fast. I trained hard to do this. It didn't come easy, but nothing worth it comes to you easily, now does it?" Israel replied. "When we get back, we will rest and then head out in the morning to start our fight against the curses and hexes of the world and those who use them for evil. Can we talk more when we stop? I'm having a hard time focusing."

"Yes, sure!" Millie replied quickly. Soon, they returned to her home and informed Chai about what had happened.

"So, you couldn't save Anong because she was hexed, and when trying to use your curse energy, it made you go overboard, which led to the death of my wife. Is that how it all happened?" He asked in a quiet and even tone.

"Yes, sir," Israel replied with his head bowed.

"Well, first, I'm happy to have my little girl back safe and sound, but I'll need time to process my wife's death. But, you know, Israel, I do not hold any grudge against you. I didn't know how much of your curse energy you could use, and I didn't know my wife was hexed, so don't let it get to you. If I knew she was hexed, I would have asked you to tell your mother to deal with it."

Israel looked confused. "Why would you ask my mother? She had never used hex magic before, had she?"

Chai looked at Israel, stunned. "You didn't know about this, young Israel? Did your parents not tell you of their past?"

"No, I never thought to ask them about it." He replied in surprise.

"I see. Well, it's not my place to tell you this. There must be a reason they didn't tell you. Well, for now, let's get some rest, and if you need to, the training ground is in the center of my house. You must remember to train properly and stay sharp and on top of your game now. If you will excuse me, I'm needed somewhere else."

Israel nodded, and Chai strolled back to his room. Apsara, who had been in the room the whole time, turned to Israel. "Thank you for saving Lady Millie, sir Israel. But I must ask you, why is Lady Millie on your back?"

"She asked me to carry her back here because she was in a weak state, so I did."

"I see. It looks like she's comfortable there. Let's get you some good food, new clothing, and some rest."

Millie scoffed at Apsara. "Lady Millie, why did you look at me like that?" Apsara asked.

Millie's expression shifted immediately. "I'm sorry. I didn't want to get down just yet. You were right. I was comfortable here, and I didn't want to move, but I didn't want to be a burden to Isy here."

Apsara was stunned. "Isy? Did you give him, I mean, sir Israel, a nickname? When did you two get that close, my lady?"

"We have a history. I used to have play dates with him as a kid for a little bit of time, and he did save my life, so I guess you can say we have always been close." Millie's face turned red. "We didn't get to spend as much time with one another, but now we have all the time in the world to get closer. Isn't that right, Isy?"

"We will be spending a fair bit of time with one another, so it would be best if we are on good terms the whole time or at least most of the time, Lady Millie," Israel responded smoothly.

"Isy, you can give me a nickname, please."

Israel thought for a moment. "I could call you Mimi. How does that sound to you, Mimi?"

Millie lit up. "I love it, it's perfect. Okay, take me to my room, and I'll get a chance to cook for you like I promised."

"No, Mimi, get your rest and eat. Tomorrow, you can cook for me."

"As you wish, Isy." Then, Israel took Millie to her room so she could rest. He went to the training center and practiced, with a thousand thoughts running through his mind. Finally, it was time to eat and get some rest."

Chapter 08

A Bored Man And An Honorable Woman

A young woman rode a stone deer down the mountain as it slid across the ground. The woman on the back of the deer looked graceful and elegant. She had a letter in her hand, with the name "Sir Charles the Hammer" written on it. She opened the letter, reading the content as her deer slowed down to a stop, flicking its ears.

"Lady Amara of the Ash family, I'm Sir Charles the Hammer." The letter read. "I'm going to get to the point of why I sent this to your family. We will need the "Thacha deer" spirit of your family once again to help fight the curses that have been a plague to our world. I understand that the deer spirit has chosen your daughter and that she's hesitant to fight because she doesn't see it as a noble thing to do."

"I hope Sir Angeni Ash can reach her and have her understand the importance of taking up this task and how it will be the noblest thing she can do. I hope to see you soon in Sir Chai's homeland, the Shadow River. I know his daughter Millie will take on this fight as well. She has become strong, and she has a competent bodyguard, a young man I've fought with for a little bit, but in that time, I know he's going to make a fine warrior. Meet with Lady Millie and her bodyguard Israel and come to my land, the Battle Lands. There's a strong cursed beast we need to handle before the others are awakened and the lands become overflowed with curses; thanks for your help in this battle. Regards, Sir Charles."

Amara closed the letter. "Millie, you're going to fight with the boars?" She said to herself. "How disappointing. Well, then, I guess I'll have to fight to make sure you don't get hurt. I don't get why that Gorilla of a man, Sir Charles, thinks just because he approves of someone, it will make me think highly of them. In my opinion, this Israel person is just another monster just like him until he proves to be different."

"The name sounds familiar for some reason." She continued her monologue as she folded the letter and tucked it away in her pocket. "I just can't put my finger on it, but it doesn't matter. Father, Arat, why must we help those who can't help themselves? Is that a way for a noble to act? I know my father is the wisest man, and he wouldn't tell me to do this if it wasn't important to it. I wish I could see it through. Is this bodyguard from a noble family of warriors? Is that why my father also approved of him? He told me he knew his father in the past; he was the only man to chance my father, but if that's the case, why would he be Millie's bodyguard and not try to marry into a noble family? Wouldn't that be a better thing to do to gain power?"

"What kind of man is this Israel person to get praise from my father and Sir Charles?" She wondered out loud as she gently stroked the deer's head. "What kind of man is his father that he could rival my father? This annoys me more. I don't like feeling left out; why didn't my father or Charles give me the information I need on this man? Well, complaining is not going to answer my questions. I'll have to find out for myself."

"I'm almost in town," she said as she observed her surroundings. "I'll go in and find somewhere to stay for tonight and meet up with them later. A lady must get her beauty sleep even though I don't need it, to be honest."

The deer spirit spoke to her. "Lady Amara, you probably shouldn't judge people you haven't got a chance to get to know. That wouldn't be wise in this war we are about to engage in. We will need them; we can't do it alone, and you just said that another proven warrior has approved Master Israel. Do you think it's good to look down on him already?"

"I will believe in him when he has proven himself to me," she responded, flipping her hair over her shoulder. "Until then, I will keep my opinions to myself. I wonder what my friend Lady Millie thinks about him. They will be meeting up with us at Sir Charles's homeland, so she should have an accurate adjustment of him by then. I wonder if it's just going to be them alone or will someone else will accompany them. If he is as capable as Sir Charles says he is, then they would be alone. No need to think about it now. I know Lady Millie and Lord Chai would do the right thing in that situation."

"Lady Amara, we are here at our destination."

"We are, thanks, my friend. So, this is the place. It's lively here. I wonder how big it is here. If what I heard from my teacher is correct, this is one of the biggest cities in the land. Well, let's see where we can find somewhere to stay the night."

She came across an old man passing by and called out to him. "Excuse me, sir, where is the nearest inn?

The old man adjusted his glasses and thought for a moment before he answered. "Oh, if you go down the street, it should be on your right. It's a little expensive to stay the night there, but it's worth it m'lady."

"Just down the street on my right, you say? Why, thank you, sir." Amara waved to him and moved forward in the direction the old man pointed to find the inn. Soon, she reached the large building. "Ah, I see this is it. Wow, it's big. Well, let's go in."

When she walked into the inn, she was stunned by the beautiful marble and gold layout of the inn and the staff full of smiles and warmth. The inn made Amara feel even smaller in size than she already normally felt. "Oh wow, this place is beautiful. I must stay here tonight." She walked up to the front desk to inquire.

"Hello. How much for a room here and food?"

The fox humanoid-looking woman smiled. "Well, hello m'lady. Welcome to The Fox Den. What kind of room would you like? We have single rooms, double rooms, family rooms, and love rooms."

"I want a single room, please," Amara replied.

"Okay, is that going to be for one night or more?"

"It's just for tonight and the morning."

"Okay, would you like to eat here tonight and in the morning?"

"Yes, please."

"Okay, that will be thirty silver."

"Alright, here you go," Amara said, taking out the money from her purse and handing it to the receptionist.

"Thank you, enjoy your stay. Also, there's a play going on later tonight if you would like to watch it. It's a shooting competition. Just go down the hall to the left and down the next hall. I hope you'll be there, it's always fun."

Amara thanked her, considering going to the play, then put the thought at the back of her mind and went to eat. Later that day, in the arena, the announcer rallied the crowd.

"Welcome, everybody! We have a match ready for all you ladies and gentlemen. We are here for the shooter gauntlet, with shooters from all around the world taking part in our event today. Let's introduce them to you all." He flourished his arm towards the contestants.

"Here we have a new contender! What is your name, young man?"

A black, close-cut young man with two six-shooters and a shotgun on his back walked up and started to speak. He caught Amara's eyes.

"I'm Marlon Patton. I joined this to test myself, and I needed something to do because I was bored. So, here I am."

"You sound like a fun one!" The announcer said in a jolly tone. "Next, ladies and gentlemen, we have a returning player, Max Tillman. He is a veteran hunter and is expected to win this match today. Do you have anything to say today?" A tall, well-built man with a heavy crossbow walked up and started speaking.

"I would like to thank everyone for coming out and wishing all the contenders here good luck in the competition today."

"You heard it, everyone. What a great man Tillman is! But enough of that, let's get to the other contest-" Before he could complete his sentence, there was a loud noise from the arena door, and a giant bull burst into the arena, rampaging. A commotion rose among the audience.

"Everyone, stay calm," the announcer said. "This is a part of the competition. Today, we are going to have the competitors fight a living beast. This monstrosity was trapped and released here and it's ready to fight for its life. I hope you enjoy the show!"

But as opposed to the audience's expectations, most of the competitors started to run away out of fear until it was only Marlon and Max left.

"We have only two contests left. Will you two fight or not?" The announcer's voice boomed across the arena, firing up everyone's spirits. Both the remaining contestants jumped into the arena, ready with their weapons.

Chapter 09

Calamity At The Arena

In the arena, the bull bashed the walls as Marlon and Tillman loaded up their weapons and leapt into the arena to take on the bull. The audience cheered with excitement and thrill as the match between man and beast began. The bull noticed the two men and charged at them, but both of them moved out of the way at the last moment. Marlon shot at the bull. That enraged the bull, and it stomped on the ground mightily, sending a quake in the ground, causing Marlon to fall. The enraged bull rushed toward Marlon, but then a crossbow bolt hit its leg, and the bull stumbled with a roar.

"Get up, kid, the fight is just starting," Max called out to Marlon. "This beast wants to kill, and I don't plan on dying here."

As the bull turned around to face Max, Marlon got up and pulled out his rifle and channeled his spirit animal, Ziggy. "It's time to turn it up a bit. Let's show this archer that we aren't novices."

Marlon became engulfed in lighting. Amara noticed and thought to herself, "Did he fuse with his spirit? I've never seen that before. Just who is this man?"

"Lady Amara, this is a unique bond that allows this user to use more power from the spirit without mastering the abilities of the spirit," the deer spirit informed her. "But it comes with a heavy price.

It's called "soul burner fusion" and it's not wise to use it unless you can make every hit count. Let's see if he knows how to use this ability, and if he can, we will need to have him on our side for this quest we are on m'lady."

"Are you sure we would need to have someone this reckless with us, Arat?"

"Yes! He will be useful. I shouldn't have to ask you to trust me."

"I do trust you, Arat; I just don't trust him, that's all."

"Don't worry, it will work out. Now, let's watch this fight; we may need to help."

The bull shot out his horns at Max. Max moved out of the way but got grazed by the horn. The bull headbutted him, knocking him into the wall. The bull went to trample him, but Marlon shot at it, electrifying it with all his might.

The bull starts stomping on the ground repeatedly, making the whole arena shake and causing it to start falling apart. Screaming and afraid, the people rushed to the exit to get out, but pillars rose from the ground and stopped them. The announcer frantically asked everyone to stay calm.

"Arat, what just happened?" Amara asked.

"It seems that the bull is an earth element user and trying to trap everyone in here. Just as I thought, we would have to join the fight.

Bring me out so I can move the pillars. It may not seem like much but it will save people from a pointless death."

"Okay." Amara grabbed her necklace and started to chant, "My family friend and protector, Arat, I summon you to fight for me and help me in this battle against the rampaging bull trying to hurt innocent people. **ARAT! COME OUT!**"

The deer spirit rose, and the pillars started to go down. The bull noticed and focused on trying to make the pillars rise again, but Marlon and a hurt Max shot rapidly at the bull. The bull shot its horns at them again.

"You're not going to get me with this again!" Max shouted as he and Marlon dodged out of the way, and he shot at the bull again. The bull horns caught Marlon and Max in the leg. The pain from it started making them feel dizzy and like they were going to faint from the shock of the pain alone.

"Tillman, you said you didn't want to die here, right?" Marlon said.

"Yeah, I won't!" Max roared.

"Good to hear. Let's make this last shot count."

Marlon's rifle started to glow. Tillman shouted, "To all my ancestors, give me the strength to slay the enemy in front of me with this one shot! I call upon you for this!"

A light flashed on Max as his heavy crossbow lit up with a heavenly glow. "Thank you for blessing me, ancestors. Alright, Marlon, let's do this!"

Both Marlon and Max shot at the bull with a monstrous amount of power. The bull tried to avoid the shot, but the ground under it trapped its feet. It caught the hit in full force, getting eviscerated on the spot. Both Marlon and Max blacked out from using so much energy.

Not sure how much time later and where Marlon opened his eyes.

"Sir Marlon, how are you feeling?" Amara asked him gently.

"Who are you?" He asked, trying to sit up.

"My name is Amara Ash. Nice to meet you. I have a request for you, will you listen to my plead?"

"Wait, where is Tillman? Is he okay?" He asked, looking around and spotted Max Tillman on the other bed.

"I am okay," said Max, getting up and walking toward him. "I will be heading home soon with my family. I think it's time for these old bones to relax. I have two sons on the way, so I need to get back soon. It was nice fighting with you. I wish you a bright future, young Marlon." Tillman clapped Marlon on the shoulder and they said their goodbyes.

As Tillman left, Amara spoke up again. "Sir Marlon, will you hear me out, please?"

"Okay, what is it that you want from me?"

"I want you to join me in fighting the curses and curse beasts on another land. Have you heard of Charles the Hammer of the Gods?"

"Yes, he was in the group with Sir Isaac, right?" Marlon's face lit up as he recalled the information.

"Yes, and judging by your reaction, you are fond of Sir Isaac, am I right?"

"Yes, he is the reason I fight the way I do. He saved my village people when I was younger."

"Well, Sir Charles asked me to join him at his home with two others to fight the curses of this world. After that fight, I want you to join me to meet the others and fight alongside us. One of them is Lord Chai's daughter, and the other is her protector. I don't have any information on him besides the fact that Charles and Chai both speak highly of his abilities. So, I guess he will be useful. Will you join in the fight?"

Marlon thought for a bit, then nodded. "Yes, I will. It must be God who made us meet like this. We were supposed to meet like this and fight together. I'll be honored to fight with you and the rest. When do we leave to meet the rest of the team?"

"We will leave when the doctor says it's okay for you to go. Thanks for helping, sir Marlon."

Amara hugged Marlon and thanked him again, and Marlon returned the gesture.

Chapter 10

Cursed Followers

"Okay, Amara," said Marlon to Amara. "I'm feeling better, and it's time to meet the rest of the group."

"Yes, you're right, Marlon," Amara nodded. "But can I ask you something first?"

"Okay, go ahead."

"Why did you agree to join me?" Amara asked with her head tilted.

"I get bored easily, and it sounded fun to me." Marlon shrugged. "I also want a chance to meet Isaac and thank him for saving my people. Plus, I want to see if I can beat him in a shoot-out between the two of us," he said with a grin.

Amara looked stunned, then laughed. "So, you want to challenge Sir Isaac to a shoot-out? I never thought someone would say that."

"Hey, what's so funny?" Marlon frowned.

"I'm sorry, but that sounds like something a kid would say," Amara tried to say in between her laughter. "You want to go against your childhood hero? I thought you were some serious, tough guy, but you're just normal, and that's funny to me."

"I'm sorry for laughing," she continued, trying to calm her laughter. "But it's refreshing. Being around my father so much, I thought most men were just straight to the point and serious all the time."

"Are you saying my goal isn't serious?" Marlon said with an air of defensiveness.

"No, I get where you're coming from. You want an all-out battle to see where you stand against your hero, right?"

"Yes, that's what I want to know. To see where I measure up with him is the greatest way to do it, so I want to know how far I am from that level of greatness."

Amara analyzed him with an interested spark in her eyes. "I like you, Marlon. I hope this works out well. Now, let's head out; we are going to meet everyone at the Black River.

"Isn't that where curses linger? That's crazy."

"I know, but it's best to meet them there. There has been a surge of cursed energy; there may be something serious going on there."

"I see; let's be off then," Marlon said, getting up and gathering his belongings. "I want to meet the other people, especially that protector, to see how capable he is."

Amara and Marlon rode on a horse toward the Black River. The journey was smooth before a tree suddenly fell in front of them with a loud crash, and a shadow ran past them.

"What was that?" Amara exclaimed.

"I couldn't see; it was too fast," replied Marlon. With a dark zoom, the shadow ran past them again. Marlon made the horse gallop faster and pulled out his gun, trying to aim at the moving shadow. Within a second, the shadow disappeared.

"Where did it go? How did it just disappear?" Amara asked in surprise.

"How did it sneak up on us? What the hell was that thing?" Marlen asked, looking around.

"I couldn't get a good look at it; the speed was too much for me to react to." Amara also scanned their surroundings.

Marlon had gotten off the horse. "I don't think it wanted to hurt us. I think that was more of a warning than an attack."

Amara nodded, looking around as far as she could. "I think you're right, but whatever it was, we might run into it again the closer we get to the Black River. That's what I assume, at least. Let's be careful."

"Right," Amari agreed as Marlon got back on the horse, and they moved forward. As they continued traveling to the Black River carefully, they were being watched from afar by someone in the shadows. They weren't aware that they were being watched, nor did they know that a major fight was around the corner.

"A few hours have passed, and there has been no sign of the shadow that attacked us," Marlon acknowledged. "It must be playing the long game, waiting for the best moment to strike. How much closer to the meet-up spot are we?"

"We will be there soon; one of the signs will be the sounds of water. I think I do hear water in the distance." Amari replied, focusing,

"So, will we wait there till they come?"

"Yes, it will be best. They should be here shortly, I hope."

"Wait, who is there? I see some people," Marlon said, squinting his eyes. "Is it them, Amara?"

Amara squinted as well. "Wait, no, that's not them. Who is that? I don't know who they are."

"Then I suggest we proceed with caution." Marlon pulled out his gun as they got closer to the two strangers.

"Put the gun away; we aren't here to fight, at least not yet." The unknown man called out.

"Who are you?" Amara shot back.

"We are followers of the cursed beast of these lands, and we are aware that you guys are with that demon, Charles the Devil Hammer," said his partner menacingly. "We want his head, so we came here to fight him. We didn't know that he would have companions, but we won't kill you here. You will tell that demon to come fight us in a different location. He can bring whoever he wants; we will be ready."

"We will settle this once and for all, and we will spread the love of the Curse around this land and the world!" the man threatened. "Come to the new location; we will fight there, and that will be where he and all who accompany him will die! So, think carefully. If you cherish your life, it would be wise for you to part ways with that devil. Come to us, to the side of the curse beast. He will lead you into the light!

"What are you going on about?" Marlon accused.

"You will have everything you desire in life when you give in to the curse," the other one continued. "Humans are flawed creatures by nature. Accept your flaws, embrace them, and become one with them. Join us and attend the blessing of the curse beast and let it become your master!"

Marlon and Amara looked at each other with calculating eyes, then back at the two men. "No, we are not interested," said Amari as they suddenly blasted the strange men with their magic, knocking them off their feet. When the smoke cleared, the duo had disappeared, and a sinister laugh was heard in the surroundings. "You two have promise, but you are so blinded by the lies you live," a deep, demonic voice said in the atmosphere. "Time will show you, and we will be there. You'll see how you were living a false life. You declared battle against us; now we will show you no mercy. Goodbye!" With ominous winds swirling around Amara and Marlon, the voice dissipated with a sinister hiss.

Chapter 11

Who Are You?

After the curse beast followers disappeared, there was an eerie feeling in the atmosphere weighing down on Amara and Marlon.

"I don't trust what they said," Marlon said skeptically. "But it didn't come off to me as a hundred percent wrong, either."

"I was thinking the same thing, Marlon," Amara agreed, caressing the horse's mane. "We can't let what they say get to us, but I don't think we need to be here right now, even though this is the meet-up spot. Those curse beast followers know we are here and may come back."

"Yes, I also think it would be best to go somewhere else for now," Marlon said.

Amara said nothing for a while, her eyebrows furrowed in thought, then spoke. "I don't know if they will come back, but they wanted us to tell Sir Charles about meeting them at the champion's battleground. Do you think we should trust them?"

"I'm not sure. I have a feeling there's something more to it, but it's just a hunch right now. Well, either way, I told you I'm going to fight. I can't lie; seeing those guys made me more intrigued to take them on. They got my blood pumping; now I can't wait to meet them again."

Amara sighed and rolled her eyes. "You sound like you're just as crazy as they are."

Marlon braced. "Don't compare me to them. You don't know either of us like that to make such a comparison."

"I'm just saying what you said sounded crazy to me, that's all," Amara said, surprised at his defensiveness.

"Enough of this," Marlon shook his head dismissively. "Let's eat something and rest while we wait for the rest to get here. We don't know when they will get here, so we might as well fill up our stomachs while we are here, don't you think?"

"Yes, I agree with you, Sir Marlon."

"Just call me Marlon and drop the sir part. I'm sure we are around the same age."

"It's a sign of respect from me to you," Amara explained.

"I get it, but it's weird to me when someone my age calls me 'sir,' to be honest," Marlon said with a sheepish smile. Amara smiled as well.

"I understand; then I will honor your wishes and just call you Marlon."

"Thank you."

"You're welcome."

They sat down on one of the rocks nearby, securing the horse.

"So, Amara, before this, what did you do back at home?" Marlon asked casually.

"Why do you ask?"

"We don't know much about each other," Marlon shrugged. "And we are going to be working together, so we should get acquainted with one another. It's for the best, don't you think?"

Amara nodded slowly. "You're right. Well, what do you want to know?"

"Let's start with the basics. What's your full name?"

"Amara Ash."

"How old are you?"

"I'll be 22 soon."

"Okay, what's your favorite color?"

Amara chuckled at the random question. "Brown and red."

"What are your favorite foods and hobbies?"

"Corn, and I like playing the flute. My mama taught me how to play, and my father loves to hear me play it, so I fell in love with playing it through that."

"That's cool. Your parents mean a lot to you, don't they?"

"Yes, they do. What about you, Marlon?"

"Well, my family is important to me. I send them money from time to time to make sure they are good. It's my job as the oldest male in the family."

"What about your father?"

"He died in my arms when I was thirteen."

"Oh. What happened?"

"A man came to our town and destroyed everything," Marlon began, looking off into the distance. "It was the second time that had happened to my people, and my father fought till the very end to stop him. It was a long fight; they exchanged blows back and forth. That fight had everyone looking in amazement; it ended with both dying. It's a story told in my hometown to this day. My father is my biggest inspiration in life."

"What about Isaac?"

"Isaac is someone I look up to, but no one is above my father. No one."

"I understand. How about you answer the other questions that you asked me?"

"Sure. I like meat mostly. Also, green is my favorite color. I'm 23 years old."

"What were you going to do if I hadn't asked you to join me?"

"Just wander around to the next thing that interests me."

Amused, Amara asked. "Do you live your life just going from place to place? That sounds so lonely and sad to me."

"I never got lonely doing it. I'm used to being alone so it's natural for me at this point."

"Oh wow! I've never met someone like you before. It's intriguing."

Marlon laughed. "Thanks. So, what should we eat?"

"If you can catch some fish, I can make us some fish and beans if you like."

"Okay, sure."

As time passed, Amara and Marlon talked more, getting closer to one another.

Suddenly, a voice called out.

"Hello, Lady Amara! I see you have made it here safely. You have a companion with you also."

Marlon and Amara looked around and saw a big man with a massive hammer walking up.

"Sir Charles, is that you?" Amara asked in surprise.

"Of course, who else will walk around with a hammer this big? I hope I didn't take too long to get here."

"It's okay. We used the time to get to know each other a bit better. Where are Lady Millie and the bodyguard?"

"They are right behind me."

That very moment, Israel walks into view lady Millie on his back.

"Hello, Lady Millie, how have you been?" Amara said, observing the humorous situation.

"Hello, Lady Amara! I've been good, what about you?"

"I've been good too. Why are you on his back?"

"Oh, I was living like a kid again, and I asked him to carry me, but let me introduce you to my friend here," Millie said with a laugh. "His name is Israel. Who is this man you have with you?"

"This is Marlon."

"Hello, Lady Millie. Nice to meet you."

"Hello, Sir Marlon. I'm Millie, and this is Israel."

"Hello, everyone. Nice to meet you all," said Israel.

"I don't think I need to introduce myself," said Charles in a playful tone. "But I'm Charles Smith, or Charles the Hammer."

"Wait, before we get any further, we have a message for you, Sir Charles. It's from the followers of the curse beast."

"What?" Sir Charles was shocked. "When did you see them? Are you okay?"

"Yes, we are fine; they didn't do anything to us. They wanted you to come to the Champions Battleground to fight. They didn't give a time, though."

Sir Charles thought for a moment, then said, "I was going to talk to you all about it, but I thought I'd have more time. They must be working on letting the cursed beast out of the Champion's Battlegrounds where your fathers and I fought it."

Amara was confused for a second. "Wait, I know mine and Millie's fathers were there, but who was the other?"

"Israel's father was there as well. It's where he met his mother."

"Wait, who is his father?"

"Isaac. His mother's name is Jazmine."

Amara looked at him in shock. "Isaac the Hunter and Jazmine the Queen of Hexes are his parents?" All heads turned to Isaac, who stood there quietly.

Chapter 12

Brotherhood Bonds

"Do you think he will meet us here, Jacob?" Ezekiel asked his partner, floating across the champion's battleground.

"Yes, Ezekiel," confirmed Jacob, looking off into the distance with a focused look. "He will be here. He wants to stop us from letting our master out so he will fall right into our trap."

"What about the other people with him that we encountered? Do you think they will be a problem?"

"I don't think so." Jacob chucked menacingly. "No, they will just be more lambs to add to the slaughter. They will also be sacrificed to our lord, and we will rejoice in his salvation. It's the perfect plan; the people he's with don't look well-trained, so they will lead to his downfall. It's best to get them to fight with him; it'll make taking him out easy because he will have to hold back and pay attention to the lesser fighters. The sooner, the better."

"I'm very aware of what kind of monster Charles the Hammer is. We can't allow him to fall into his blood lust, or it will be the end of us."

"Is he that scary?" Jacob raised his eyebrows in doubt.

"Let me tell you about the past battle with him and his team, and you will understand why I'm doing all of this. A while ago, he and his companions came to battle by my father's side. That's where I got my first-hand glimpse of what power looked like. I had never been so scared in my life of another human, and it wasn't just him. The rest of his brothers what just as strong. I was relieved that they were fighting with us and not against us. Everywhere they went, bodies flew."

"They did this with the coolest, lifeless looks on their faces," Ezekiel continued as Jacob listened in silence. "It was as if it didn't faze them at all that they were killing their fellow men, and then it all changed. My lord warned me to leave, or I would have been killed as he was. Suddenly, the battlefield turned black, and I couldn't see anything. In the blink of an eye, I saw them fighting my people and killing them one by one. My lord told me again to run and that he would protect me. He told me that he would get trapped, but I would live to release him one day."

"So, I ran as they stormed my kingdom. They killed my father, the king, my mother, and my sisters. They almost killed me as well. Isaac shot at me, but I kept running. My lord gave me the strength to get away. He fought them to the end, but they trapped him here, and I am here to release him. After I got away, I found this black crystal. It was from him, and I heard his voice in it speaking to me."

"His voice? In the crystal?" Jacob asked in surprise.

"Yes. He told me to kill the ones who trapped him and bring him one of their bodies so that he would take it as his own. He said that when he returned to this realm, he would bring my family with him and bring back my kingdom that I would rule. He told me that I would lead everyone into the day of the Blessing of the Curse. People will learn that the curses of the world are not sins but enlightenment, and I would be the one to bring in that period as the king of all. After hearing that, I knew what I had to do. I had to kill the enemies of my lord and save everyone in this cruel world."

"I see," Jacob said, pondering over Ezekiel's story. "But why do we wear these masks?"

"We wear them to protect us from the evil of the world. The spirits possess the user and take over the way they think; then, people think they have to fight curses to save the world when they have given in to the real enemy of humanity. But the time has come for the final battle. My lord will be freed, and then we will go free his brother in other parts of the world. After we take out Charles and his friends here, we will get Isaac and the rest. Then, we will go after the Gobeullin So-bangdaethe or Goblin Fire Squad to capture the curse beast of the winds. Do you understand why we are on the side of the righteous now?"

"Yes, I do. Let's prepare for this fight coming up."

"Yes, let's get ready, my brother."

Over at the Black River with Israel and friends, Amara questioned Charles about Israel.

"This doesn't make sense to me. How can Israel be the son of Sir Isaac and Lady Jazmine when Lady Jazmine gave up her humanity?"

"She regained it by giving up her ability to use hexes, but she and Isaac had to pay a price. Jazmine was reborn; that's why we call her Jazmine now; that wasn't her birth name."

"What is her birthname?"

"We can't say; we all forgot it, and I think that was meant to be, but none of that matters now." Charles waved his hand as if shooing the topic away. "We need to come up with a battle plan to fight the cult of the cursed beast."

Millie interjects. "Aren't they called the followers of the cursed beast?"

"That's what they call themselves, but we don't. The lead was a prince of a fallen kingdom whom the curse beast attacked in the past. We fought to allow the people to escape. But it became one of our biggest blunders ever because during the battle, the cursed beast somehow got a hold of the prince and made you think we were the real villains. He has been following him and gaining followers from people who are down in their lives or just plain crazy. They probably think you aren't battle-trained to go against them. They don't know your parents prepared you for this all your life. Well, we don't know about you, sir Marlon; you're a wild card here to me."

"Well, how about I fight Isaac's son here to show what I can do?"

"Wait. I want to join you, Marlon. Is that okay with you, Israel?" Amara stepped in.

"Sure, go ahead."

"I just had a great idea. How about all three of you fight Israel?" Charles suggested. "I need to see how you all will fight against someone as strong as he is. I think it will be a good test. Millie, will you join them against Israel?"

"I don't want to fight," Mille replied with pursed lips. "But I do think we need to get our team chemistry together, and I have a feeling this fight is going to be important."

"Okay then. Everyone, let's do this battle simulation before our big fight. Get ready!" With that, everyone got into position, preparing themselves.

Chapter 13

Friendly Fight

"Fight!" Charles' booming voice rang out.

Marlon pulled out his guns, Millie pulled out her staff, and Amara summoned Arat. Marlon asked Israel, seeing that he pulled out no weapon. "Are you not going to get ready?"

Israel shook his head. "I'm in my fighting stance already."

Amara and Marlon looked confused. "Are you not going to get your magic ready? Or anything?"

"I don't use magic," Israel explained. " I'm just a bare-hand fighter. I can use curse energy and ice from my curse spirit animal."

"People don't fight barehand anymore, and how do you have a curse spirit?"

"Enough with the questions. Fight me, and you will have all your answers."

Within a second's notice, Marlon started shooting at Israel. Amara sent Arat to take on Israel's head, and Millie cast a fire blade and rushed in to attack Israel. Israel dodged the array of bullets from Marlon and kicked Millie's sword, shoving her into Arat. He ran towards Millie, hitting her in the gut and kicking her, making her fall to the ground.

"Sorry, Millie," said Israel, "You're a healer, and I know to take you out first, so you make winning this much harder."

Two loud bangs indicated that Marlon shot at Israel again. Amara ordered Arat to trap Israel in the ground, but Israel jumped in the air and sent out an energy blast. Marlon got out of the way at the last second, and Amara blocked the energy blast.

"So, he can fight from a distance. I'll make him regret not fighting with his whole arsenal." Amara said to Arat. "Arat, before he lands, shake the ground and catch him when he falls. If we let him keep dictating the battle, he will knock us out cold."

"Amara!" Marlon called out. "I need you to trap him in the ground and I'll make this shot count."

"Were you reading my mind?" Amari responded in surprise. "I got you."

Millie got up and started casting a spell. Israel raised a dust storm and blocked everyone's site. As the dust cleared, Israel was nowhere to be found. Suddenly, a roar came from the forest nearby, and Israel came into view, along with a beast he was fighting.

Marlon noticed the speed they were fighting at, shock and alarm taking over him. "Amara, that's the beast that we ran into earlier. I remember that speed; let's help Israel out."

Millie cast a fire cage spell, trapping Israel and the monster in one area. Israel grabbed the monster and slammed it on the ground. "Now!" He shouted.

Amara trapped it in the ground, and Marlon aimed for its head. Amara and Arat shook the ground and wrapped up the monster, burying it in the ground. It was as if all of them were reading each other's minds and making moves in accordance with the rest. Marlon pulled out his shotgun, aimed it, and blasted the beast, blowing its head off.

Charles clapped. "Well, well, you all worked together brilliantly. Even though that's not what I expected, but it proves even better that you will be a great team. It helps show what we will have to work on for this fight. Let's go; we need to do more training before the battle."

"Before we do, your name is Israel, right? The son of Isaac the Hunter?" Marlon asked, clearly not having moved on from the earlier topic.

"Yes, we went through that already. Is that a problem??

"No, your father is someone I have great aspirations for. He saved my people; I'm in debt to him. To have his son right in front of me fighting the same fight must mean something."

"I see," Israel observed. "But I could tell in our battle that you wanted to challenge me. Are you trying to use me to see how you would measure up with my father?"

"Yes, that was the reason for challenging you."

"I see. How do you think you did?"

"I don't have an answer. You weren't going all out, and neither was I, so it's hard to tell."

"Then will have to find out later, right?"

"Right." The air was charged with a mix of admiration and excitement.

Amara spoke up. "Israel, you said you can use curse energy, right?"

"Oh yes," Israel turned towards her. "I can; I'm a curse eater. Do you know what that is?"

Amara and Marlon had a shocked look on their face. "Yes, I know what that is, but I thought it was not real," said Amara.

"Yeah, me too," Marlon agreed. "So, you can eat curses and gain strength or new abilities from them?"

"Yes, but I also have an ice spirit. I just can't use its magic abilities, but I can use its ice power. I can blend both the spirit and curse beast abilities with my power; I just have to balance it so I don't favor one side more than the other."

"Why?"

"Because if one gets too strong, it will take over. Too much curse energy will allow me to be taken over by the curse, which will be bad."

Millie looked at Charles with concern. "Should we allow Israel to fight? There's a lot of curse energy that could be around; what if he ate it all? Wouldn't that become a problem?"

"I see where you are coming from, Millie, but we will need him, and he has learned to control it. As a curse eater, he is supposed to eat curses at some point, so he should be able to eat a curse beast with no problem and still have control of himself. This upcoming battle will be a great test. If it gets too out of hand, then we will have to kill him with your purifying magic. It's counter to his curse energy; we will have to make sure he doesn't get to you first because if you get hurt, we won't be able to kill him if things get out of hand."

"Kill him?" She asked in utter shock. "Why do we need to take it there?"

"Because a curse eater is a danger to our world if he gets corrupted by the curse. In Israel's case, it may be easier for him, too, because he can power up his spirit energy to contain his curse energy. It's all we can hope for right now. I was hoping it to be a while before you had to fight them but I still think you can win this. I'll be there to help out as well. It will take three days to get to the champion's battleground. We will take a week so we can get you guys working together better along with me."

Israel had a serious look on his face as he said, "This sounds harsh."

Millie responded seriously. "We're all going to be ready with your help; I know we can win this battle, Charles."

Chapter 14

The Champion's Battleground

Part 1

"Come on, Israel, focus your energy. You must get control of it," Charles urged Israel. "Allow yourself to control the curse energy and spirit energy within you."

Israel focused on improving his control over his powers. He focused and listened well. The curse and spirit started to talk to Israel.

"We can feel you trying to tap into our power. You are not ready for it yet; you haven't consumed enough curse energy to train your mind and spirit. You will have to give in to yourself fully, which means giving in to the curse as well as the spirit energy inside you. We understand you are having second thoughts about this, but it's for the best that you do this. Once you do this, you will become much stronger and gain a portion of the curse eater's true power, along with a portion of spirit energy. Let us start becoming one with you."

"How will I know I am ready for this now of all time?"

"You have been ready, you just haven't accepted it because you think you're not ready for the responsibility of it all. Accept this fate and make the most of it here and now, Israel!

"I will not run. I will accept what will come. For accepting this power that belongs to me and only me, I will not lie to myself anymore," Israel said with determination. "I was scared the moment I killed Millie's mother that I wouldn't be able to control this, so I've been trying to fight without it because I don't want to hurt another innocent person and make someone else lose their loved one." As he said all this to the spirits inside him, he started to glow blue, gray, and black. His aura expanded and caught everyone else's attention.

Millie and Amara started chanting, "Israel, you can do it!"

Israel's surroundings became covered in his aura. Suddenly, everything went back to normal, and two markings of wolf fangs appeared across his eyes. His teeth sharpened, and his aura glowed around him as if he were a new person.

"Charles, look at Israel!" Mille called out.

"You look like you did it."

"Yes, I did," responded Israel. "I have a new level of control over my power, but I didn't get much stronger. It's noticeable, but it's not a big change. I'm grateful to God for this chance. Now, let's continue so we can win this fight; I'm ready for it."

"Good. Everyone, how are you feeling?" Charles turned and surveyed the rest of the team.

"I'm ready," said Amara.

"I've been ready even before this training started," said Marlon.

Millie said, "I'd like to practice a little longer, then I'll be ready."

"Okay, keep going. We will need you to be the best you can be, so keep at it, Millie."

"I will, Sir Charles. I just need today, and I will be ready for the fight ahead."

Israel walked up to Millie. "I will oversee your remaining training to ensure that you're ready. I don't want to go back to your father with another death."

Millie blushed and said, "Thank you, Israel. I don't want that either, for any of us. I pray you continue to watch over me like you do now."

Israel nodded and sat down as Millie started to train. Millie thought to herself, "I can't be the weak link. I can't let everyone down here. I'm the one who hasn't done any fighting, so I have to make sure I'm up to par with everyone."

She continued to train as hard as possible and Israel watched over her. After she finished, she walked up to Israel, "Thanks for watching over me, but I couldn't help but feel like your mind is heavy. What is wrong?"

Israel looked at Millie with a serious face. "I still have a hard time forgiving myself for killing your mother."

Millie smacked Israel on his head. "Israel, I told you I forgive you. Stop letting it haunt you. We have to fight tomorrow; you can't let this take over your mind."

Israel nodded. "Thanks, Millie, I needed to hear that. I know I need to have my head clear, but I couldn't let it go until I knew you truly forgave me."

"I do. I already have, and I told you to stay by my side. That couldn't happen if I kept this grudge against you."

"So, now I can truly let it go."

They smiled at one another for a bit before Israel said, "Let's get some rest. Tomorrow is a big day for us all, Millie."

"Yes, let's go rest."

Everyone gathered, ate, and went to sleep, mentally preparing themselves for the battle ahead. The next morning came, and Israel and company headed to the champion's battlegrounds.

"How long will it take for us to get there?" Israel asked.

"We are close to it. Is everyone ready? Not just physically, but mentally and emotionally ready." Everyone nodded their head.

"Good, we will be there soon."

After a little while, they reached the champion's battlegrounds and saw their enemies. Jacob spotted them first and said, "You see that, Ezekiel? I told you he would come, and it seems like his companions decided to die with him today." He raised his hand and summoned an army of people. Israel and everyone looked around.

"What is this?" Marlon said. "He summoned an army of people out of nowhere, what is this level of magic?"

Ezekiel heard him and smiled. "This is the blessing of the curse you were offered to join," he said in his demonic voice, an eerie feeling falling over the scene. "But you sided with the wrong side. Here is where you will die today. But don't worry, I will bring you all back as a part of our army so we can free our lord and take over this country and then the world!" Jacob and Ezekiel laughed in pure evil tones.

Before anyone could register anything, Ezekiel shouted, "Kill them!"

With a mighty roar, the curse warriors charged towards Charles and his group. He looked at his team and said urgently, "Israel, me and you are on the front lines, so anyone who gets behind us, Marlon can finish them off. Millie and Amara can give us cover from afar. We can and will win this; let's go!" With a battle cry of his own, he led his team into battle.

Chapter 15

The Champion's Battleground

Part 2

With Charles the Hammer's war cry beating down on all of them like a true hammer, Israel and Charles went running into the battle scene. The other side also ran forward, their screeches charging the air with electricity. Every single person present was now in battle. Marlon pulled out his six-shooter and aimed it one by one at every warrior trying to surround Israel and Charles.

Millie rapidly shot fireballs at the warriors while Amara blocked in any arrows that came their way from the enemy archers. The sounds of weapons clanking against each other and the warriors crying out were making the sky itself shake. Charles backed up against Israel, scoping out those they were fighting. He pointed at Jacob and Ezekiel, getting Israel's attention. "We need to get to them fast before they can get more of these things out."

"Let's do it," Israel replied with determination. Without him noticing, Jacob disappeared all of a sudden. The cursed wolf called out to Israel. "Pay attention; one of them has gone missing. You need to let me take over here for a bit so we can track him."

Israel saw Millie flying backward, not knowing what hit her. Heart stopping to a standstill, he gave in to the cursed wolf. His eyes turned black, and his curse markings glowed, showing a subtle yet noticeable shift in his personality shows.

"Good, I'm in control now." A deep voice reverberated from Israel's mouth, but it wasn't Israel's voice. "Where did you go?" He looked around, seeking Jacob. With the help of the cursed beast's power, he made out Jacob's silhouette, even in his invisible form.

"There you are!" Israel said in that deep, manic voice. He rushed over to Jacob's location and struck him in the face. Jacob let out a painful cry, suddenly becoming visible. "How the hell did you see me?"

Israel looked at him with a sinister grin. "Wouldn't you like to know?" Jacob swung at Israel, but he dodged his fist and jumped out of the way. With lightning-fast movements, Israel was suddenly as nimble as a cat, even with all his muscles. He punched Jacob once again, knocking him backward.

Jacob laughed with mirth. "You are pretty strong. But I've been hand-to-hand fighting for years; you can't beat me. Let's have a one-on-one fight, just you and me, young pup."

Israel bent his neck to the side with a light cracking noise. "Bring it on," he said, with the dark madness shining in his eyes.

In the next second, both of them jumped at each other and dashed around, fighting at breakneck speed. Their peers watched in awe while trying to fight their own opponents. Marlon shouted, "Ziggy, help me keep my eyes on them so I can help Israel out."

Ziggy powered up Marlon and started to track Israel and Jacob. Amara and Millie combined forces, the air crackling with power around them as they covered Charles as Marlon ran to help out Israel. Millie, with the wind swirling around her and her eyes glowing as if she were something inhuman, cast a firebolt at the group of curse warriors. The mighty bolt blew the warriors away before they could overpower Charles.

"Arat, go!" Amara yelled out, and Arat glided through the air towards Charles. Charles raises his hammer and banged it on the ground, reminding everyone why he was known by the intimidating title of Charles the Hammer. The ground cracked and opened up, swallowing the cursed warriors. "Die, you unholy abominations!" Charles roared and swung his hammer once again, making waves of hash wind blow the warriors further into the ground. The sounds of the quaking ground and rapid winds were enough to make any common man's heart explode with fear, but they were trained warriors fighting the battles of their lives in the midst of the storm.

Ezekiel summoned a new group of cursed fighters; this time it was an army of cursed animals, both land and flying. "I see you having fun with my Warriors so I thought I would change it up," he snarled at Charles and the new cursed creatures rushed to attack. Millie jumped to Marlon's and together, they shot down some of the flying beasts. The mangled faces of the beats were something they had never seen before. A dark mist rose from each of them as they fell to the ground.

Amara sent pieces of the earth flying at the animals as Charles went ran up to Ezekiel, swinging his hammer and hitting him square in the face. The scream that came from Ezekiel sounded as if a human and an eagle were screeching together. The sound grated on Charles' ears but he stood his ground. Suddenly, a cursed tiger attacked him from behind. Charles fell forward but twisted around immediately, his hammer swinging around to meet the tiger in his face.

As Charles was focused on the tiger, Ezekiel blasted him from behind. More beasts rushed toward Charles down, and the flying beasts seemed to be taking over Millie and Amara. Some of them even caught up with Marlon and attacked him, knocking him down. Ezekiel laughed with glee as the team seemed to be losing, but not just yet.

Marlon jumped back up to his feet. "Don't celebrate just yet, demon. I'll finish you off fast and get back to helping Israel. Ziggy, it's time for fusion!"

Marlon fused with Ziggy and shot powerful blasts at the flying beasts, destroying them in one hit. The cursed beast copied his moves and became a cursed angel. Marlon grinned, "Getting serious, are we? That's what I like." With another mighty war cry, he dashed towards the angel. It shot its pointed feathers towards Marlon but he dodged and kept running until he was face to face with the cursed angel, landing a hit on its shoulder. "What's the point in fusing if you're still going to be just as weak?" He taunted as the beast snarled in pain and shot out more feathers, but Marlon was quick.

With a second's distraction, the beast caught Marlon in his chest with its claw, ripping a painful cry out of his lungs. Amara appeared by his side as if she had magically transported, and with fire dancing in her eyes, she blew the beast into smithereens. Marlon breathlessly stared at her in awe but she shouted, "Go! Find Israel!"

Millie and Amara joined forces again and blew the cursed animals backward, though both were breathing heavily now, the weight of the battle pressing down on their shoulders. Their hair coming down in a mess and dirt smearing their face, none of them showed any signs of giving up. They kept the beasts at bay and away from Charles so he could finish off Ezekiel. On the other hand, Israel and Jacob fight like great blocks of iron clashing against each other.

"What's your name, young pup?' Jacob called out.

"Israel." The manic grin had not left Israel's face.

"I'll remember that. It has been fun but this needs to end now." In a flash, Jacob hit Israel with full force, making him fall to his knees, then kneed him in the head. His aura was getting darker, and he picked Israel up and slammed him to the ground, dragging his body across the ground and throwing him into trees. "It was fun, even though it was short-lived," said Jacob in his booming voice that carried all the ill intentions. In the blink of an eye, Marlon shot him in the side but Jacob merely budged. "You're not worth my time, get out of my face."

Marlon laughed as he pointed behind Jacob. "I may not be, but I don't think you're done with him yet." Jacob turned around and immediately fell back as Israel hits him in the face. Beaten up but still standing, Israel's dark grin widened.

"You should have made sure I was dead." with blow after blow, Israel set on finishing Jacob off. Jacob roared, " Enough of this! You won't mock me, you little mutt!"

Israel looked at Jacob with a cold look in his eyes. "Then shut up and fight me." Jacob lunged at him again and dark sparks flew off into the distance as they collided. Marlon charged up his shotgun. Israel landed a hook at Jacob then kneed him and slammed him to the ground, making the earth shake.

With his breath frozen in his lungs, Marlon took aim and shot, leaving a hold in Jacob's chest. Israel's spirit animal said to him, "Let me take over! I can freeze him and then the impact will break him."

"Okay, but I want his curse energy," said Israel and immediately, his curse marks turned blue. He hit Jacob, freezing him completely, then kicked and sent his pieces flying around.

Marlon ran up to Israel, panting. "Is it over?"

Israel touched the broken pieces of Jacob and absorbed his curse energy, getting back up.

Marlon asks again. "Are you okay?"

"Yes, his curse energy isn't going to affect me until I get some rest. Can you run fast?"

"Yes, with Ziggy's help, I can."

"Good, we should get back in a couple of minutes."

Charles and Ezekiel weren't done fighting. Amara and Millie had lowered the number of curse beasts and warriors with their attacks. Ezekiel belts out, "No! It can't end here. Master, please help me!"

A mysterious, haunting voice sounded in the atmosphere. "My child, I'll help you. Take my power and destroy your enemies."

Out of nowhere, a black lightning bolt shot out and hit Ezekiel, disappearing inside him. Ezekiel turned black and turned into a monster with four arms. "Now you all will die!" He roared.

Charles stepped back and told Millie and Amara to get back and focus their attacks on Ezekiel. He raised his hammer. "By the gods, give me the strength to smite my enemy before me!" His hammer started glowing. Charles called Millie to get ready to purify him and told Amara to attack Ezekiel head-on. "We will have to make time for Israel and Marlon to come back so we can fight him together."

Charles raised his hammer again and shouted, "Heaven Armor!" Suddenly, he was covered in heavenly armor. "It's time to end you once and for all." With a loud cry, he and Ezekiel clashed with one another, trading blows with one another. They continued to fight, making shock waves as they sent blow after blow.

Amara turned to Millie frantically. "We need to help or this will never end."

"I'll get a purification spell ready, you send your spirit animal to help Charles." Amara followed Millie's orders and sent Arat to help Charles. Arat hit Ezekiel in the back but it didn't move him. Arat stood back and tried to make the ground under Ezekiel trap him, and Charles landed a mighty hit on him but Ezekiel stabbed him in a split second.

Millie gasped and shouted, "Sir Charles!"

"I will be okay," he grunted in pain. "This little cut won't stop me from getting home to my family."

Ezekiel had taken notice of Millie trying to make a purification spell. "No, you will not finish that spell. You little witch, I will not let this be the end!" Ezekiel blasted Millie with a wave of cursed energy and there was a loud band. Ezekiel flew backward and Ezekiel looked down at Millie, writhing on the ground in pain. "Millie!" he shouted. "Are you okay?" Millie did not respond.

Ezekiel got up from where he had land and yelled. "What did just do? Where is that cursed spell I used? It should have killed you!" Israel turned around and looked at Ezekiel with hatred in his eyes.

"I ate it. That's what a curse eater does. I eat curses; I'm going to eat your master as well." His voice was low and threateningly deep. Marlon and Amara ran toward Millie as Israel turned toward Ezekiel.

"Millie, I need you to trust me, okay?" He called out but Millie barely responded with a groan. Israel, Arat, Marlon, Amara, and Charles stood against Ezekiel, hitting him from every angle.

"Millie, now!" Israel shouted and Millie, with whatever consciousness and energy she had left in her, shot the purification spell towards Ezekiel. He yelled from the pain of the spell as he started to disappear. Israel punched Ezekiel and started absorbing his curse energy.

Suddenly, there was a hissing voice all around them. "I've found a new host." An abundance of curse energy blasted into Israel. Israel went flying back in slow motion, dark tendrils of energy creeping around him and his going completely black. Everyone screamed and shouted, but there was no response from Israel, the magic warrior.

THE END

Author's Biography

Rakim McGhee is a story town author following his dreams telling the stories he wants to tell

Author's Note

Thank you all, even if one person reads my book. I want to thank you for supporting me, this is the first book I've ever made. I know I still need to grow as a storyteller, but I'm happy to get this out, and I hope you enjoyed it. I was worried while working on this book but it helped me realize how strong I am. I found my calling, and I found God again with this, and I now walk with His armor.

I want to not only thank everyone who reads this but tell them to go for their goals in life. It doesn't matter what your age is or if you're well off or in the dirt; make each day yours. You can do it. I know you may not believe in yourself; I didn't at first, either. Nothing can happen until you believe in it first. Just remember, I believe in you, so please do yourself a favor and reach your true greatness. That's enough from me; thank you. I hope you continue to support me. Until next time!

MUCH LOVE,

RIM

www.ingramcontent.com/pod-product-compliance
Lightning Source LLC
LaVergne TN
LVHW061037070526
838201LV00073B/5075